THE BEAUTY AND THE BEAST

THE BEAUTY AND THE BEAST

ALANA ALBERTSON

Bolero
Books

The Beauty and The Beast
Copyright © 2016 by Alana Albertson.
Cover Designer: Aria Tan of Resplendent Media
Cover Photography: Wander Aguiar
Cover Model: Zack Altland & Joli Irvine

Bolero Books LLC
11956 Bernardo Plaza Dr. #510
San Diego, CA 92128
www.bolerobooks.com

please return to your favorite ebook retailer and purchase your own copy. Thank you for respecting the hard work of this author.

AUTHOR'S NOTE

To instantly get a free full length book, Deadly Sins, sign up for my newsletter: **Free Book**

This book is dedicated to all the amazing wounded warriors who have sacrificed so much to protect our country and our freedom.

EPIGRAPH

Love doesn't need to be perfect, it just needs to be true.
Beauty & the Beast

THE BEAUTY AND THE BEAST

Isabella—Grady Williams is a national treasure, the youngest living Medal of Honor recipient, America's scarred superhero. With tattooed arms sculpted from carrying M-16s, this bad boy has girls begging from sea to shining sea to get a piece of his action.

When my father squanders away my college fund, I make a deal with this dirty-talking Devil Dog—I will pretend to be Grady's girlfriend for the Marine Corps Ball, and my dad will write Grady's war memoir.

Grady is fearless. Hell, this badass jumped on a grenade to save his fellow Marines! As much as I crave him, I refuse to allow myself to become addicted to a dangerous man who will detonate my heart.

Grady—Isabella Cuesta is an angel who can see

beyond my mangled skin, a pawn used to repay her father's debt, a woman who makes me feel like a man instead of a monster.

But I no longer believe in fairy tales.

She's mine until our contract ends. I'll take her hard and rough, listen to all her hopes and fears, lay down my life to protect her.

This beauty will never let herself love a dangerous man like me—a man who has killed, a man who runs towards gunfire, a man who never backs down from a fight.

But without her love, I'm not a man—I'll remain forever a beast.

GRADY

I blasted the volume on the television, trying to drown out the noise from a goddamn frat party down the street. Loud music, water splashing in the pool, girls laughing maniacally —the sounds of people enjoying their lives. At least the racket sounded better than the clamor running through my head.

The ricochet of gunshots, my friend screaming in pain, his agonizing cries during his last seconds of life —that was the clatter that racketed through my skull. And I could never turn it off, not even when I slept.

Why had I been the one to survive the battlefield? The survivor's guilt was almost worse than my physical scars.

And now, I'd been deemed a fucking war hero. At twenty-five years old, I was the youngest living Medal of Honor recipient. I'd met the President—even shared a beer with him in the Rose Garden.

He'd invited me to be the guest of honor at an upcoming Marine Corps Ball in Hawaii that he would be attending. Sounded great, but I needed to find a date worthy of meeting the leader of the free world. I couldn't exactly bring one of the porn stars I'd recently fucked to meet the President.

My commander-in-chief had given me one piece of advice—get an education. Sounded great in theory, but only one of my eyes worked, dirt from the attack was still embedded deeply in my wounds, and the burns on my skin itched so fucking badly that I spent my free time gouging my own flesh off. And those were just the physical problems. Mentally, I was a complete fuckup. I couldn't shake the premonition that I was headed for some sort of *Final Destination* fate, doomed because I'd cheated death. The littlest noise made me as skittish as one of the wild dogs in Iraq. I couldn't focus on any task for more than a minute, and I struggled daily trying to heal from my injuries.

College wasn't an option for me now because the thought of sitting in a room filled with people scared me more than jumping on that grenade. I wouldn't have time to attend even if I wanted to. For the past two years, I'd endured intensive physical therapy, nonstop burn and facial reconstruction surgeries, not to mention PTSD treatment, which was the most painful experience of them all. And I'd be too drugged up to focus. My docs forced me to try a bunch of meds that gave me at worst a limp dick and at best massive headaches and sleepless nights. I'd done group therapy, individual therapy. Fucking bullshit. I'd rather get a skin graft than talk about my feelings.

The only benefit from this fucking hell that was my life was that every time I had left my place, I'd been swimming in a sea of pussy. Women couldn't wait to get a piece of me, like being fucked by me made them some type of patriot. But that was all they wanted. One night riding a hero, and by morning they were quick to bail, find a man who didn't look like he escaped from the circus, a man who could take them to a fancy dinner without freaking out and having a flashback. I enjoyed all the attention at first, but sometimes I yearned to find someone who actually liked me for me.

The voices down the block grew louder. I peered out the window and could see the party raging, a bunch of rich, spoiled college kids dressed like superheroes.

Kickass. I could do this. The old me hated costume

parties or anything with a theme—I'd much rather get wasted with my buddies. But since I looked like Frankenstein now, masks suited me just fine.

I pulled out my razor because I didn't want my beard scraping against my mask. I rarely shaved because I couldn't stand the sight of myself in the mirror. I'd never get used to looking at my face.

A freak. A monster. A beast.

My face was now split in two. On one half, my eye drooped, my skin sagged. On the other, I looked like the man I used to be.

Now I had a face only a mother could love. Too bad my mom had abandoned me years ago.

Could anyone ever stand the sight of looking at me every day? Or would I always remain some type of novelty—a patriotic pity fuck?

I dug out my favorite costume—the Hulk—stained my body with green camouflage paint, pulled on my shorts, and tugged the latex disguise over my head.

Normally, once I told a woman my name, she'd start fawning over me, and thank me for my service by sucking my cock. But tonight I wanted to try something new. I was up for a challenge. I wanted to keep my scars and my identity a secret. Maybe I'd be able to meet a girl tonight who would get to know me first before judging my appearance and my actions.

Someone sweet, caring, and classy. Someone I could invite to the Marine Corps Ball. A woman who wouldn't be scared of getting to know the real man behind the mask.

ISA

I logged into my student services account and stared blankly at the screen.

HOLD—Please contact registrar

A warning in bright, capitalized red letters. What on earth was going on? My tuition was supposed to be deducted directly from my account every month. I'd taken all the money I had earned while on *Dancing under the Stars* and created a tuition trust. No one else had access to the funds except my father because he was the trustee. I shot my father a quick text to call me. There wasn't much more I could do at this point—it was Saturday night and the university was closed. I briefly considered trying to find my login for my trust, but assured myself that I was panicking and should just wait until I heard from my dad.

Now what was I going to do tonight?

My nervous hand shook as I clutched my cell phone. What was it again? Swipe right if he didn't look like a psychopath and left if he posed shirtless in a mirror selfie? These guys didn't have a single friend in their lives who could take a decent picture of them?

Forget this.

I deleted the app. How pathetic was I?

Pretty pathetic, actually.

After living in the public eye for so long, I didn't trust anyone. Once a man found out I was a former reality star, he treated me differently. Like I was some fame-hungry whore, good enough to hook up with but not to date.

But I refused to hide anymore. I'd spent the first year post-spotlight cowering from the media, cringing every time I saw my name on the gossip sites. "Makeup-free former reality star Bella Apple-baum indulges in fattening treat." Cue the mean tweets.

At least interest in my life had died down. I stopped using my stage name, moved, and changed my phone number and email account. I was now living as Isa Cuesta, struggling twenty-three-year-old

THE BEAUTY AND THE BEAST

college senior. Bella Applebaum, America's ballroom dancing sweetheart, had disappeared.

Sighing in frustration, I reached for my Kindle—maybe I'd just throw myself into the latest bad boy romance novel.

Just as I perused my book choices, my phone lit up.

Marisol.

My gut clenched. My goodtime girlfriend was no doubt looking to recruit a wing woman.

Marisol: Phi Delt Party at SDSU. Get ready.

My fingers typed frenetically.

Isa: Sorry, not my scene.
Marisol: Too late. I'm on my way!

Great. I hated parties. A bunch of drunken frat guys and vapid sorority sisters would get wasted, hook up, and then take their walks of shame the next morning. I preferred seeing a live band downtown, catching the latest indie flick, or checking out the newest ethnic restaurant. But I did need to get out. Though it was mid-summer, I was burned out from having a full load of classes all year. I spent my vacation teaching barre, doing research for my psych professor, and studying for my GRE exams. I deserved one night of partying.

My long, dark hair was still damp from the shower. I sprayed some Moroccan oil on it, dabbed my face with concealer, lined my green eyes with a metallic gold pencil, and applied nude lipstick and mascara. One glance in the mirror and my confidence came back. Despite being the offspring of an alcoholic author and a tragic, old-school Vegas showgirl, I prided myself on being natural, normal, and real, which I considered quite an achievement having spent my late teens in La La Land. Four years ago, my life had been so embedded in the Hollywood scene— filming my show, attending premieres, posing for photo shoots, raging at after-parties, and gloating at award shows. Thank God I'd escaped and regained my sanity—though I definitely had some scars from my time in the limelight. I now lived in San Diego, which while still technically SoCal was a welcome break away from the L.A. party drama.

As I picked out an outfit, my doorbell buzzed. I opened the door, and saw Marisol standing there, dressed as Catwoman, clutching a shopping bag in her hand. Her brunette ombré hair was pulled back and her heavy makeup featured winged cat eyes, a pink nose, and sparkly whiskers.

Oh, hell no.

I rolled my eyes. "The animal shelter is closed."

"Funny, Isa. It's a superhero-themed bash. Don't worry—I hooked you up, girl!" She rummaged through the bag and pulled out a red wig and a black leather catsuit.

At this point, I had two choices—either go along with Marisol and embrace wearing this getup, or run like hell and lock myself in the bathroom. But she'd never take no for an answer.

"You want to go as twin Catwomen? That's super lame, Mari."

She let out a purr. Well, I had to give her credit for getting into character.

"No, silly. You'll be Black Widow. You know, from *The Avengers?* Come on, get dressed. My parents are watching Paloma. Please don't make me go alone."

Well, I had to go now; Marisol rarely had a free night between school, work, ROTC, and watching her child. Paloma was her adorable three-year-old daughter, who Marisol swore was the result of a one-night stand with a famous rock star. Marisol adored Paloma, never regretted her choice to have and keep her, and never sued for child support. I'd always encouraged her to contact the father; he had the right to know he had a child. She swore that she'd tried but that he had vanished.

"Fine, but we're not staying long. And don't you

dare leave me alone with some sleazy guy while you make your rounds."

I studied the costume and ran my hands along the rubbery material. I squeezed my body into the suit, slicked my hair under the wig cap, and slipped my feet into my shiny black pumps. Costumes and makeup used to be part of my daily life. I shuddered from the tightness of the wig cap, the familiar ache in my calves from the heels. I'd always felt trapped, like I couldn't breathe. Not anymore. These days my wardrobe consisted of tank tops, jean shorts, and flip-flops, and my beauty routine involved hardly any products other than sunscreen, tinted moisturizer, and lip balm.

But sometimes, late at night, I would fantasize about dancing a slow foxtrot, held in tight frame by a strong partner, our legs melting together until we moved as if we were one.

I closed my eyes and inhaled a calming breath. After a few seconds floating back down to reality, I opened my eyes and smiled—I could pretend to be someone else at this party and hopefully no one would recognize me. It would be nice to try to find some common interests first before someone judged me from what he'd read in the tabloids. This costume could allow me to break out of my shyness. My father was a huge *Avengers* fanatic and dragged me along to all the movies. I think he secretly wished he'd had a son, but after my mom died I was all he had left. At least I could relate to Black Widow's character—she spoke Russian and had been brainwashed into thinking she was a ballerina. I learned some Russian from my old dance partner and had been forced to dance by my mother. But deeper than our superficial connection, Black Widow always emanated a sense of loss and loneliness. And that was something I understood intimately.

Though we both went to University of California at San Diego, this frat was at San Diego State. SDSU was way more of a party school, but for tonight, that was fine by me because I needed a change of scenery. I climbed into Marisol's beat-up sedan, and we left pretentious La Jolla for the laid back College Area of San Diego. I took a moment to center myself and appreciate the beauty of my surroundings. Turquoise skies without a hint of smog, accented with the deep green burst of treetops. Though I was less than three hours away from LA, I felt a world away from Hollywood's haunting famous sign, which lured young people from around the world into the deadly cog of fame.

"So, I was reading *Star* magazine, and you won't believe who Pasha is dating!"

Great, I was trapped alone in an interrogation

vessel with Marisol. The perfect opportunity for her to force me to talk, since normally I would either hang up on her, not reply to her nosy texts, or just walk away. In her defense, this was the only way I would really answer her questions. "I don't care. And I told you a thousand times that those stories are all fake. I'm sure he just had his publicist plant some stories so he could stay relevant." She never believed me, but I spoke the truth. According to the tabloids, I had hooked up with every partner I ever had on *Dancing under the Stars*. Which was totally not true, but I was sure those rumors no doubt contributed to the way people treated me.

"Even so. Aren't you the least bit curious about your old partner?"

"Nope." And I wasn't. That jerk never gave me the time of day though I used to have the biggest crush on him. He was older, already a ladies' man, and I was just an inexperienced teen. He tossed our partnership aside when I needed him the most. Even worse, he hadn't defended me when the press started making crazy allegations about why I'd left the show. Most days I doubted that he ever really cared about me.

I gazed out the window, trying to erase the past from my mind. The show destroyed my life, devastated my soul, and detonated my family.

"I'd do anything to find out what Dax was doing,

even though I barely knew him. But he vanished." She placed her hand on mine, and squeezed it. "Sorry I brought it up." Marisol turned up the radio, and some pop catastrophe filled the air.

Her smile faded. Though she completely owned her choice about sleeping with Dax and she loved her daughter, I couldn't fathom how hard it would be to be pregnant and not even have had a chance to tell the father. Every choice has consequences.

I didn't blame Marisol for being curious about my former life, a life that the media made out to be so glamorous, when it was actually soul-sucking. She was one of the few people I confided in about the real horrors of my dance with stardom. And I planned to keep it that way.

Marisol parked her car a block away from fraternity row and we walked toward the house, the chaos from the party spilling out on the street. The usual suspects milled around the lawn—a full range of Supermen, Batmen, Thors, Captain Americas, and Iron Men. I also counted a dozen Catwomen, a few Wonder Women, a Batgirl, a couple of branches of Poison Ivy, a Supergirl, an Elektra, and even a Harley Quinn. But as far as I could tell, I was the only Black Widow. This place looked like a Comic-Con after-party.

We made our way into the house, and despite

Marisol's vow not to leave my side, before I could even blink she had stalked off toward a Joker sporting a winning grin. Joker apparently knew Catwoman, evident by their overly friendly embrace.

I watched them flirt for a few moments until Marisol motioned me over to join the group, attempting to lure me with a skinny Aquaman as bait, but I refused. When I shook my head, Marisol mouthed, "Be right back," and Joker placed his arms around her and they went to the basement.

Great. We hadn't even been here for the full length of a song and I was already on my own. I grabbed a red Solo cup, poured myself a rum and coke, and prayed to be anywhere but here.

Batman groped at Poison Ivy on the sofa; Superman and Wonder Woman exchanged heated words in the kitchen. Spider-Man played a friendly game of beer pong with Green Goblin. Ha! Apparently no one did research on their characters' enemies and allies. This sucked—my hopes of meeting someone interesting were dashed as I took in the usual "let's get wasted" party scene. The cacophony rang through my ears, and the scent of weed, sweat, and beer wafted through the house. I stepped out to the brown and patchy back lawn, no doubt a casualty of California's drought, and inhaled the eucalyptus-scented air. A DJ spun tracks while a bunch of coeds splashed around in the pool, Wolverine grilled burgers, and there was a Marvel versus DC superhero volleyball game going on. Still not my idea of a good time.

I retreated to a corner of the yard overlooking the majestic canyon, away from the chaos, and nursed my drink.

After people-watching for a bit, a green flash caught my eye. No, not San Diego's famous sky streak. Opening the sliding doors from the frat house was a man wearing a mask—his skin was tinted green, and he wore ripped purple shorts.

The Hulk.

At first glance, I was convinced he had one of those muscle costumes on, padded fabric to make him appear to be strapping. But no, oh no. This man was massive—arms twice the size of any other man's at this party, broad shoulders, rock-solid abs. But unlike the Hulk, this imposter's entire body was covered with tattoos, which were hard to decipher since they were obscured with body paint. I tried to avert my gaze but I couldn't—I was drawn to him, like a magnetic force. He oozed confidence, the way he stood there assessing the environment, like he owned this house, when he was clearly out of place. Who was this man? No way he was a frat brother.

Was he looking at me? *Don't be silly, Isa.* He was

probably just scanning the full scene to see who would be the lucky girl to go home with him tonight.

I volunteer as tribute! I snickered to myself. Too bad this wasn't a *Hunger Games* party.

A few girls stopped to check him out, not that I blamed them. He looked at the ground, and his hand reached into a rose bush where he plucked a single red bud. Wow, that was fast; he was probably already hitting on one of the girls inside. I felt like I was on one of those stupid *Bachelor* shows—hundreds of desperate women, one hot guy, and nothing to base any romantic connection on besides a fleeting first impression.

I finally drew the strength to turn away and wipe the drool from my face. One long gulp of my drink and I would be fine. But seconds later, a looming shadow appeared at my feet, and the intoxicating smell of cedar, vanilla, and cinnamon made me realize I wasn't alone.

"Welcome aboard, Russian," a deep voice said in a sexy drawl.

I looked up and the Hulk hovered above me—the bloom in one hand and a beer in the other.

Ay dios mío, he was breathtaking. Well, a mask covered his face, but his body was incredible. Incredible Hulk indeed. He could be the Hulk's stunt double —no special effects needed.

I steadied my nerves and downed my drink. "That's not Hulk's line. Iron Man said that."

He let out a laugh, or maybe it was a growl—the sound was muffled under that mask.

"*Avengers* fan? I've been searching for a Black Widow all night. Here, this is for you." He handed me the rose.

My belly quivered, pleasantly surprised by the sweet gesture. The only time in my life I'd ever received flowers was after a big dance performance, and those were from my father.

"Thanks, that's very sweet of you." His tattoos were in focus now—the first one I could decipher was a huge USMC emblem on his right biceps. Whoa, a Marine—well, that explained his body. There was a quote in Latin, *Semper Fidelis.*

"Nice tattoo, Devil Dog. Always faithful?"

The Hulk sat next to me, his green skin shone in the moonlight. "Yes, ma'am. Do you speak Latin? Or have you dated a Marine?"

I definitely detected a deep Southern accent. "No, I've never dated a Marine. I know it's the motto of the Marine Corps. My father is a Marine. Well, once a Marine, always a Marine; he retired before I was born." And then he met my innocent mother. Young, beautiful, from a rural town in Mexico. But my father rarely talked about himself; he preferred to tell other people's stories. "And no one speaks Latin. It's a dead language."

"I know that, Natasha Romanova. I was making a reference to *Iron Man 2*."

"Yeah, I get it. My dad's dragged me to all the movies. My name's Isa. What's yours?"

He paused. "Bruce Banner, but you can call me Hulk."

This guy couldn't even tell me his real name? Strike one. I immediately put up my guard. Probably another player, but with a body like that, who could blame him? His hand brushed against my thigh, and my core heated up. I couldn't help but stare at his shorts as the huge bulge stared back at me. Looked like his chest wasn't the only part of his body that was massive.

"Okay, Hulk. So what's your job in the Marines?"

"I'm a grunt, ma'am."

I loved the way he said *ma'am*. I was so used to SoCal surfers, frat boys, and Hollywood types that I was charmed by his politeness. I just hoped it wasn't fake.

"Cool."

"So you don't hate military guys like most of the girls in San Diego?"

I wasn't imagining a bitter edge to his voice. But it was refreshing that he didn't seem to hold his opinions back. "No, I don't. I actually admire any man who would risk his life for his country. Being in the military isn't a job, it's an honor." Much more honorable than my former life in the spotlight, existing to please people, making money off my appearance, fakeness, dishonesty. I shuddered remembering the older pictures on my now defunct Instagram account. Thank God, I'd changed my path. Even if it hadn't been by choice.

He leaned in closer to me and squeezed my hand. "I'm glad and, well, shocked you think that. It means a lot to me, thank you. How about you? Do you go to SDSU?"

"No. UCSD. But I want to apply here for grad school." I studied Hulk's body. He had a deep scar on his right shoulder, and even though it was covered in green makeup, I could tell that some of his skin was mottled and puckered.

Should I ask him about his obvious injuries? Would that be rude?

His strong hand covered mine; the strength of his grasp excited me. I imagined this man dominating me, a fantasy that I'd never had the pleasure of experiencing with the passive pretty boys I'd dated.

"Isa, you're the most beautiful woman here. This party really isn't my scene, and I'd like to get to know you better. Let's get out of here."

Well, that was quick. So much for my romantic Southern gentleman. "What did you have in mind, Hulk?"

Before he could reply, a loud boom detonated nearby. A blinding flash of light streaked the sky, the shimmer of multicolored fireworks overhead.

Hulk instantly dropped the beer, glass shattering under us. Before I could react, he threw me to the ground and flung his frame on top of mine, his body shaking, a labored breath emanating from his mask.

What the hell? "Get off me!" I yelled, pounding his chest with my fists, shards from the bottle scraping my skin.

I suffered through a few seconds in silence, praying he would move, but he just clung to me like cling wrap. The pressure on my chest tightened, but no matter how hard I tried, I couldn't push him off. I writhed under him, my face pressed to his green chest.

Finally after what seemed like a few minutes, he rolled off of me and sat up, his hands shaking. Sweat beads adorned his chest. A crowd had now gathered around us, probably trying to make sure I wasn't being raped. Had a firework gone off? Oh damn—was that some kind of war flashback? How insensitive was I?

"You okay, honey?" some girl asked, glaring at the blood on my costume.

"I'm fine." I sat up, brushed myself off, and picked up the rose he'd given me, now crushed on the grass. Luckily the glass had given me only superficial cuts.

Hulk plowed through the crowd and ran off.

"Wait!" I screamed after him, but he was gone. I dashed out of the backyard, through the house, and onto the front lawn. Hulk stormed down the street.

"Hey, wait up!"

He didn't turn his head, and I wasn't even sure he heard me. He just kept on walking and made a right at the end of the block.

I should've let him go—he obviously wanted to be alone and had just had some sort of trigger—but I wanted to make sure he was okay.

I flicked off my heels, threw them and the rose into my purse, and ran down the street. I finally caught up to him as he was using his key to enter an apartment building.

I slowly placed my hand on his shoulder. "Hey, I'm sorry I yelled. I was just a little scared. Do you want to go back to the party with me?"

His head turned to me. I wished I could rip that damn mask off of his head and read his expression. "No," he said, his breath labored. His hands fidgeted, and then he crossed his arms.

Cars whizzed by the street, drowning out our silence. This guy was obviously going through something. Sure, I'd just met him, but after failing to detect all the signs of my mother's depression, I'd made a vow to never turn my back on someone in need.

We stood there in awkward silence. "Did you have a flashback?"

"Something like that. I'm fine."

He did not seem fine. His voice was shaking and he flinched at my touch.

"It's okay. I mean, my mom used to have episodes. I'm not judging you. Do you want to talk?"

"I said I'm fine. Just need to relax. I don't do well in big groups of people. I should've never gone to that party." He exhaled and his shoulders dropped. Then his chin tilted up, and he placed his hand on my back. "But then, I would've never met you."

Ah. The charm was back.

"I'm glad you went."

His lips grazed my ear. "Come upstairs with me."

Whoa, arrogant much? In any other situation, I would've run for the hills. Despite my reputation in Hollywood, I'd never gone home with a guy whom I'd just met. "I don't think going up to your place is a good idea."

He leaned into me, his firm hand tracing mine. "It's the best idea I've had all night."

His body was now pressed into mine, and I could feel his rock-solid cock poke through his shorts.

Ah, damn. I knew what he wanted—and I'd be lying to myself if I said a part of me didn't ache for him too. Lust aside, I wouldn't be able to forgive myself if I walked away from him now. I needed to be assured he was okay.

But I wasn't stupid—I recognized that I didn't know this man. I wanted to just talk to him, some-where safe, somewhere public. "Do you want to grab some coffee with me? There's a café a block away. Or if you're hungry, there's this great hole-in-the-wall Thai restaurant around the corner."

"I'm not going anywhere but home. And you're coming with me."

Damn. I should've told him off, but the ache between my legs compelled me to stay.

"But...I don't even know your name." Nor had I seen his face. I refused to walk away without getting a glimpse of the man behind the mask.

His fist clenched. "Are you coming upstairs or not?"

I took a deep breath. "Okay, but just for a bit. My friend's at the party."

His head tilted to the side. "I didn't see you with a friend."

"Yeah, well, she ditched me when we got there."

"Some friend."

Hulk had a point. Even so, I took out my phone and texted Marisol my location just in case I ended up in a bad situation.

We walked upstairs to the second floor, and he opened his apartment door. His place was masculine and modern—IKEA-style black furniture, a huge flat-screen television, and a small balcony with a tiny barbecue. Instead of the room smelling musty, like most guys' rooms I'd been to, his smelled like lemons and pinecones. It was immaculate. He must've either had a maid, which was unlikely, or he was a complete OCD neat freak. The creative slob in me was impressed. I sat nervously on the sofa and he stood in the kitchen, watching me.

What on earth was I doing? "What's your name?"

He just shook his head. Okay, I was in a strange apartment with some psycho, nameless Marine who just had some war flashback. I'd probably end up in a ditch, the subject of a future episode of *Dateline*. Well, at least my dad would get the opportunity to pitch the story about my disappearance and murder to *Vanity Fair*—a boost and paycheck he needed for his slumping writing career and mounting bills.

"Okay, Hulk. Are you okay? Do you want to talk?"

He didn't say a word, just opened the refrigerator, and grabbed two beers. He handed me one, then leaned against the granite kitchen island, his hips jutting out, and I couldn't help but stare at the bulge in his shorts.

I took a swig of my beer, the bitter taste filling my mouth. Awkward. I didn't know what to say, but I didn't want to leave. In addition to my immense attraction to this man, I wanted to know his story. I had to see if his face was as breathtaking as his body.

I looked at him. "Will you take off your mask for me?"

He grunted. "Only if you take off your clothes."

Whoa. Did he just say that? Who did this guy think he was? With that body, he clearly had no problem getting women to spread their legs for him. Was this his game? Play the damaged vet card to gain sympathy from unsuspecting coeds?

Not that he needed a ploy. This man was incredibly hot. Hands down the best body I'd ever seen. Like one of those fitness models who graced the covers of my romance novels.

"No way, Devil Dog." I gathered my purse and stood up. "Look, I made a mistake. I wanted to make sure you were okay, but you're clearly fine and all, so I'm going to see myself out. It was nice meeting you."

I walked toward the door, but he grabbed my wrist. Before I could protest, he pressed his body against mine, shoving my ass against the black granite countertop. His huge cock pushed against my crotch, and my core ached.

"Don't leave." His voice was deep, sexy, guttural, as his fingers traced my side.

I was unable to speak, my adrenaline spiking. I could race out of here, slamming the door on any hope of taking this further. Or I could stay and see this night through. Our interaction had started out so promising. He'd given me a rose, seemed to be interested in more than just a hookup, even though he'd asked me to leave the party with him after we'd just met. Maybe I'd read him wrong and he'd been about to ask me out on a date? It wasn't his fault that an ill-timed firework ignited and ruined our moment. Why should any connection we might have become a casualty of his pain?

At the same time, he did seem cocky, which turned me on yet frightened me. He'd clearly had many hookups and knew what to say to get a woman into bed.

Rebelling against my common sense, I kept my feet planted on his laminate tile floors. He pulled off my wig and wig cap, my hair cascading in my face. His hand undid the zipper of my catsuit and peeled it off my body, kneeling to slip it off my feet.

I did nothing to stop him.

He stood back up and unhooked my bra, his rough

hands teasing my nipples. I gasped when his fingers slipped into my black lace panties, which within seconds fell to my ankles.

He didn't ask me if it was okay—he acted as if he owned me, which was sexy and scary at the same time. Lust waged a battle with my brain. My body yearned to be touched, my head urged me to flee, yet my nerves sensed no danger. I felt strangely safe. Like I could tell him no or leave at any time.

I stood in front of him, buck naked, as he eye-fucked my body. After giving him more than enough time to stare at me, I squeezed his shoulder and lowered my voice. "Take off your mask."

For a few seconds he didn't move. His hesitation tortured me.

Then, without a word he ripped the mask off and looked me dead in the eye. His shoulders back, his chin up, as if he was standing at attention.

I battled the urge to recoil in horror. A wave of nausea hit me, and despite my best effort, I let out a gasp.

Ay dios mío! What the hell happened to this man?

GRADY

IRAQ—TWO YEARS EARLIER

The blazing Iraqi heat incinerated me, my flak jacket serving as my own personal oven. The pounding in my head was relentless, and it wasn't just from the popping of the nearby AKs. I flicked a sand flea off my chest and took a swig from my hydration pack, but the few drops of water did little to quench my thirst. The dehydration, bug infestation, torching sunbeams, and constant sounds of gunfire ensured that the sandman had refused to pay me a visit for days.

My men and I were clearing houses. I was a fucking grunt in an infantry unit, the backbone of the Marine Corps. A human sandbag. I'd joined hoping one day to become a scout sniper—and more than ever wished I were prone on some building offing these terrorist motherfuckers before they assassinated my brothers. At least I was happy to have my friends by my side—Trace, Preston, Diego, Beau, and Rafael. These men were my brothers—and out here, the dirty water that bound us together was thicker than blood.

One more house. We'd already cleared two and this was lucky number three. This one was two stories and even had a fucking roof. I threw the purple magic cloud in the air to disorientate the enemy and the smoke grenade detonated. "Let's go!"

Diego went in first, and we hustled behind him. The rancid air smelled like a putrid mixture of gunpowder, shit, and sour goat's milk.

"Clear," Trace yelled out after he checked the first room. Luckily, the second room was vacant also.

I sprinted upstairs, my men close behind me. As we turned the corner and entered the room to the left, the distinct popping of the enemies' AKs went off.

"Get down!" I crouched in the corner of the room, desperate to get the fuck out of here. Alive. With all my men. Diego returned fire, clouding the room with gunfire and smoke.

And that was when I saw it flying through the window.

A fucking hand grenade. Right next to Rafael.

We were all about to fucking die.

"Grenade!" I screamed. "Get the fuck out."

I'd always believed that you could never predict how you would act in a deadly situation until the Grim Reaper knocked at your door. Nothing could've been truer in that moment.

I was about to die. All my friends were about to be blown up by these motherfuckers.

Not on my watch.

Limbs shaking, tears choking in my throat, I flung my body down on the grenade preparing to shield my men from the blast.

Rafael tried to drag me away, but I remained still, praying for mercy and a quick death. I counted the seconds until my life was over—until I would meet my maker.

A stream of gunfire ricocheted through the building, headed toward Rafael, who had refused to leave my side. His heart-wrenching scream echoed through this shanty house as his head split open before my eyes, his brains splattering on my cammies.

"No!" I screamed. It was too late—despite my sacrifice, my best friend was dead.

Boom!

Agony ripped through my chest, my heart spontaneously combusting, as I let out a desperate scream.

The world was black. I thought I was dead.

But I wasn't fucking dead; I could never be that lucky. I was alive, trapped in my own body. Cries desperately trying to be heard, tears burning my skin, every nerve in my body short-circuiting, lying in my rotting flesh. Metallica's song, "One," played on repeat in my head. The smell of ammonia and bleach filled the white room. Maybe I'd been committed to an insane asylum.

My only working eye made out the image of a man in a white coat walking into the room, a reluctant smile hiding the pity on his face.

"Sergeant Williams, I'm Dr. Evanson. You're at Walter Reed Medical Hospital. You've been in a coma for three months; we didn't think you'd make it. Congratulations, son, you're a hero."

It was a smile I would get to know intimately, for that same condescending smile would end up gracing the face of every politician asking me to pose for a photo, every active duty Marine praying they wouldn't end up like me, every woman I propositioned.

It was a look that said simultaneously "Thank you for your service" and "This poor bastard."

ISA

*G*uilt from my initial reaction to his injuries tormented me.

At first I was determined not to stare at his face, horrified that he'd be insulted by my reaction. But the second his face came into focus, I held back a sob, and a lump grew in my throat.

The right side of his face was mangled, taut raw flesh accented with blue and red scars. His jaw was uneven, and his right eyelid slumped, filled with what must've been a glass eye. The remnant of his ear was dappled and twisted. But the other half of his face was clean-shaven, handsome and rugged—a bright turquoise eye, strong chin, black hair shorn in a Marine Corps high and tight haircut.

Flashes filled my brain, stored images I must've

retained from newsreels and graphic war movies. Had it been a roadside bomb? An outmanned firefight? Some type of chemical attack? I wouldn't ask him. For now, I was content with the trust he had shown me by unveiling his scars.

"I guess I should've gone to the party as Two-Face," he said, his voice somber.

"No, you're beautiful. You make a sexy Hulk." I caressed his face, my fingers tracing its divots. "Plus, then you'd be DC, and I'd be Marvel. We would've never had a chance."

He let out a small laugh, but flinched at my touch. "You've seen me now. You're free to go."

This was my chance to end this night safely and in control.

Or I could get wild—do what I'd only ever read about in my books.

Cut loose.

I'd always admired those women who owned their sexuality, like Marisol. Indulged in pleasure without any guilt or shame. I wondered what it would be like to live in the moment.

I was picky, but I still had needs, and right now I needed some action—and sadly these days the warm glow from my eReader was about the closest that I felt to having any heat radiating on my body. But even the artificial afterglow of one hot night with my latest romance hero did little to warm my heart. After all, I hadn't had sex since my last relationship ended. I missed everything about being around men—their masculine scents, their non-subtle eye fucks, their rough hands. At least my book boyfriends were gorgeous, witty, and incredible lovers—but most importantly, they wanted more from their heroines than just a one-night stand.

And I was sure this man wasn't looking for anything more than a hookup.

Isa, put on your clothes and get the hell out of here. This is not you. You are responsible, conservative, and goal-oriented.

Faced with the opportunity to indulge in my fantasy of hot, wild sex with a hunky alpha male, I had to admit that the reality of the situation made me realize how rigid I'd always been.

But somewhere deep in my soul I wanted to lose myself in this damaged man, give him pleasure to alleviate his pain, experience ecstasy and release.

And maybe he could heal me too.

The heat between us rose, and I erased the distance between us, like two magnets being drawn together.

I traced his face with my fingers, running the tips over his lips. Rough, wild, and dangerous. As he remained still, my hands explored his incredible body

—rock-hard muscles, deeply embedded scars, and intricate ink. All making him look like the sexiest badass alive.

He bit his bottom lip; his pupil dilated.

Hungry.

Ravenous.

Intense.

His chest heaved, and the sight of this raw, ferocious man before me sent a shock between my legs. I ached for him to relieve the tension that consumed my body.

I pressed my palm onto his chest, the green body paint staining my hand. "I want to stay. I want you."

Damn, did I just say that? My words betrayed my will.

The left side of his mouth widened into a grin, although his right side remained frozen in time. With one arm, he clutched my ass and wrapped my legs around his waist. I gasped as his mouth covered mine. His lips were neither soft nor sweet—they were hard and hungry. The length of his cock and the hair on his chest let me know that, unlike my previous boyish lovers, I was about to be fucked by a real man.

There was no turning back. I needed this Marine inside me in the worst way.

His kisses were out of control. I'd never been kissed like this before, like I was an oasis in the middle of the desert. His mouth tasted minty and hot, and his manliness intoxicated me. He awoke a latent desire in me, summoning my inner wildcat. I kissed him back, kissed him everywhere. His mouth, his lips, his neck, his scars. My hands explored his insanely ripped body, stroking him like he was my personal sex toy. I gripped his hair and dug my nails into his back, kneading him closer to me, never wanting to let him go.

I'd always been the good girl, living vicariously through my friends' hookups, only indulging in my fantasies in the safety of my mind. Whether it was from a place of fear or control, I had never allowed myself to fulfill my desires. But tonight, with this nameless sex god in my grasp, I made a silent vow to not hold anything back. I was going to let him fuck me like it was the last night of the world.

He shoved my ass on the countertop as his hands worked their way down my body, his mouth suckling on my nipples. A moan escaped my lips. I could feel my pulse beat in my core, and the thought of his hot tongue working its magic between my legs was almost enough to make me orgasm. I arched my back as his fingers teased my pussy, his thumb rubbing my clit.

"Oh, yes," I moaned. "Just like that. Don't stop."

He groaned and dropped to his knees, his lips

ALANA ALBERTSON

teasing me, showering my warm, wet flesh with kisses. He pushed his finger, first one, then two, deeper inside me, twisting and turning, and I gasped. I ran my fingers through his hair, wanting more of him, more of his tongue, more of his fingers. One wicked glance up at me, and he buried his face in my pussy. Ohmigod. His tongue danced around me, licking me into a frenzy as sensations of bliss pulsed through my body. Glancing down at this sex god going to town on me, my legs now wrapped around his neck, I felt so naughty. I didn't even know this guy's name, so why did he feel so right?

"I'm gonna lick you until you come all over my face, baby."

Ahh. His tongue worked its magic against my clit. A rush of pleasure coiled in my core, rising and falling, desperate for release. My pussy throbbed and a wave of ecstasy exploded through my body, the sweet freedom making my body tremble.

He looked up at me as he slowly stood up, his one eye hungry with desire. I kissed his neck, careful to give his wounds extra attention. I wanted to take my time, explore every inch of his body. It would take me a lifetime to memorize it, but I might only have this one night. I kissed his chest, lavishing love on his nipples. I massaged his hard flesh, all the while studying the scars and tattoos on his muscular frame.

What was his story? Where was he from? What had happened to him?

I licked my way down all eight sections of his abs to his happy trail before dropping to my knees. His shorts were still on, so I unbuckled his belt, pushed down his boxers, and his huge cock stood at full attention. Wow, it was beautiful—thick, long, and harder than concrete.

I took a moment to look up into his eye and smile. I wanted him to know that I wasn't taking pity on him—I wanted this, I wanted him. He was the hottest man I'd ever seen, and the scars only made him sexier to me.

He bit his lip and ran his fingers through my hair. My mouth opened and my lips created a seal around his cock, and he let out a heavy grunt. I licked the head and did my best to take him deep. I'd never really enjoyed giving blowjobs, even though I'd wanted to please my ex-boyfriends. But pleasuring the man standing above me, his sculpted body naked for my eyes only . . . for the first time in my life, I truly appreciated how sexy this act was. How giving him this pleasure might take away even a small bit of his pain.

He groaned and his eyes hooded. "That's it, baby. Suck me hard."

I obeyed his command, locking my eyes with his. I

took him deeper, sucked harder, my hand wrapped around the shaft. I needed to give him pleasure, make him need me.

I wanted to taste his hot cum in my mouth, but he pushed me off of him. I rose, never losing his gaze. He threw me over his back like he was some caveman and I was his possession, opened his bedroom door, and tossed me down on the bed.

He reached for a condom, ripped open its package, and rolled it on his cock. I touched his hand. I had so many questions, but before I could open my mouth, his body hovered over me. He asked me if I was sure, and I gave him an affirmative nod and a breathless yes. He exhaled one deep breath, parted my thighs and slid inside me, setting my every nerve on fire. He grabbed my hips and pushed deeper. I was so wet for him, my pussy clamped around his cock.

"Baby, you're so tight."

I moaned and he pulled out and thrust fully inside me. He pinned my hands behind my head and fucked me.

"How do you want it, baby?"

Lust had taken over my mind. I had only one goal —to completely lose myself in this moment, and have him lose himself inside me. "Hard and rough."

"My kind of girl. Spread your legs, baby, that's it."

He pushed my legs back so my knees were near

my neck. I arched my back and he thrust harder, faster, rougher, my pussy stretching to take him, take him deep. His left hand clutched my ass, pulling me into him, ensuring my clit received the indirect stimulation that I craved.

"So fucking sweet. Show me how much you want me."

And I did. I writhed under him, working my hips, rocking back and forth for him, like I was performing an intimate dance just for him.

"That's it, baby. Take me deep." He squeezed my hand and pumped deeper, rubbing my nipples. He was so huge I was astounded that I wasn't in pain, but I was loving every to-the-hilt second of him being inside me.

He released my hands, pulled me up so we were facing each other, and wrapped my legs around his waist. His mouth sucked on my tits, and I almost came again, but he slowed the pace, edging me like I'd only read about in my romance books. "Not yet, sweetheart. You don't come until I say you come. Ride me now; don't hold back."

My hips swiveled around his cock, my clit rubbing against him. My ecstasy came in waves, but every time I was close, he somehow managed to change his pace, not allowing me to go over the edge, to end this moment.

He slapped my ass and pulled my hair. "God, you're so fucking sexy. Good girl. Do you want to come?"

"Yes." I ground deeper into his body, savoring his touch, his silent intensity, his beautiful cock. I was so wet, so hot, every cell in my body bouncing in euphoria.

"Say it. Tell me what you want."

"Make me come."

Mouth on my nipples, he grasped my hips in both hands and pounded me down on his cock, finally setting me free. I let out a scream as he held me close, rocking my body through my orgasm. A final deep thrust and he let out a guttural groan. Then I collapsed in his arms.

We cuddled for a few minutes, our bodies intertwined in the now green-stained sheets. The silence was awkward; I didn't know what to say. Despite my assurances to myself that I could handle this random hookup, a wave of guilt crashed down on me. I couldn't believe I just had sex with this man.

I didn't even know his name.

I wondered what this naked man next to me was thinking.

My fingers traced the scar on his shoulder. "What's your name?" I whispered.

"Grady," he said in a low tone.

Grady? Holy shit! As in Grady Williams? The war hero? I'd read a magazine article about him. He couldn't be. But Grady wasn't a common name.

I popped up in bed and stared down at him. "You're Grady 'The Beast' Williams? The youngest living Medal of Honor recipient?"

"Yes, ma'am."

Ay dios mío!

There had been a before picture of him in the magazine and I remembered thinking he was so handsome, but I hadn't recognized him tonight underneath all his scars.

"Oh my God! You're a hero. My dad's, like, obsessed with you." So obsessed, in fact, that my father dreamed of writing Grady's war memoir. My mind raced, trying to recall all the details of the article I'd read. Grady was legendary. This badass had thrown his body on a hand grenade to save his friends' lives.

He rolled away from me and sat up on the side of his bed. I sat next to him and noticed his hand was shaking. "I'm not a hero. I was just doing my job. Fucking bullshit that I was given an award to remember the worst day of my life."

This guy blew my mind. "Are you kidding me? You saved the lives of your friends—you could've died.

You threw yourself on a *grenade*, Grady. How are you not a hero?"

"Anyone would've done it."

Um, okay. Not true. Hell, my old dance partner once used my body as a shield because he didn't want to get wet in the Splash Zone at SeaWorld. Worse yet, he split the second my life fell apart.

"So that's why you freaked out back there?"

I wanted to feel something, connect on more than a physical level. I'd always been fascinated with warriors—I'd written a paper for my classics course on "The Ancient Greek Hero"—it was about time to get to know the modern version.

He didn't reply, not that I expected him to, and instead stood and walked into the bathroom. I heard the water turn on and I lay back down, paralyzed in bed.

I'd just been fucked by the man the press hailed as "America's Bravest Beast."

GRADY

I scrubbed the green body makeup off my chest, the saccharine sweet aroma filling the shower—at least it smelled better than the coppery scent of blood. I flashed back again to that night, the image of my buddy's brains strewn on cammies before my body imploded. No matter how many fucking therapy appointments I had, no matter how many bottles of vodka I drank, no matter how many girls I fucked, every time I closed my eyes, I was right back in Iraq.

Black Widow, AKA Isa, however, had done something that no girl had done since I'd been back. She didn't abandon me after one of my episodes. In fact, she chased me down to make sure I was okay.

I had been shocked she ran after me. Her presence

calmed me down faster than I normally would have had I been alone.

I never realized how much I needed someone to care about me.

After forty surgeries, flat-lining twice, and excruciating rehab, I definitely had my share of freak-outs. Fireworks, of course, were an obvious trigger, but lesser things set me off too. The sound of dogs baying in the night, the scent of diesel, the crush of a huge crowd. After a few too many flashbacks, my ex-girlfriend flipped out, packed her bags, and left without looking back. Fuck that bitch. All those nights in the hospital, dreaming about her, and she left me the second she could conjure up an excuse. But I knew the truth—it wasn't because of my nightmares; it was because she couldn't stand to be dating a circus freak. Her new boyfriend was one of those collegiate pretty-boy types—lean body, shaggy hair, looked like he could be an Abercrombie & Fitch model. He could blend in at her country clubs, where I'd always stand out like a mutant.

But I couldn't blame her for not wanting to deal with my problems. Even in *Beauty and the Beast*, at the end the Beast turns into a prince. I would always remain a one-eyed jackass.

I stepped out of the shower. By now, I'd given Isa enough time to flee the scene of the crime. No matter how she tried to hide it, I saw her look of disgust when she saw my face. And this girl had recognized my name—she'd definitely find an excuse to bail.

Back in the bedroom, I was shocked to find her still naked, curled in a ball on my bed. I'd expected her to already be dressed, phone and keys in hand, ready to make an exit.

She was so fucking hot and I'd seen her somewhere before, but I couldn't remember where, which wasn't surprising with my memory loss. Looked like an angel—well, the Victoria's Secret kind. Her long hair cascaded around her chest, the wisps barely covering her nipples. Her green eyes were the color of kryptonite, and her tanned skin was completely smooth. And her body—full, natural breasts, tiny waist, and a tight, round booty.

I recognized her, but where the fuck from?

Before my injuries, I never forgot a face, which was why I knew I would've made an excellent scout sniper, my dream job. But I would never qualify anymore with one eye and a spotty memory.

Her pupils appeared dilated and she pulled at her hair. "Hey."

Yup, she was definitely looking for a reason to bail. "Hey. I'm going to drive you home." I walked over to my dresser, threw on some boxer briefs, gray sweatpants, and a T-shirt.

Her shoulders slumped. "Oh, okay. I hoped I could hang out for a bit."

Kickass. Maybe I'd read her wrong and she was up for another round. Maybe she even could look past my face. "Okay. You want some pizza?"

She hopped out of bed, and I stared at her naked ass as she walked into the bathroom. This chick was fine as all hell. She looked like a movie star—she definitely didn't want to date a guy who looked like the Terminator.

When she came out of the bathroom, I handed her a T-shirt of mine, hoping that when she finally grew sick of looking at me, she'd leave it behind and her scent could comfort me for a few days.

God, when did I become so fucking pathetic?

That was easy—the night my face was blown up.

She went into the living room, slipped on her panties, and sat down on the sofa.

I warmed up some slices of Round Table pizza. The silence was awkward. I shouldn't have told her my fucking name. Now she'd probably interrogate me and I'd have to relive that night. Not that I could ever forget it—it played on an endless loop in my head.

I sat down next to her and handed her a plate.

Her lips widened into a smile. "Thanks. So, just wanted to tell you not to worry about what happened at the party. I'm a psych major, and I want to apply for a doctoral program in clinical psychology after I graduate. I'm a really good listener if you want to talk."

Great. I fucked a shrink. Well, a future shrink. This chick wanted to lay me down on a sofa and instead of riding my cock, force me to confess my deepest sins. Most women tried to fix men anyway, but this woman was going to school for that shit. I didn't need her to pity me.

"I'm good. Talking never solves anything."

She pursed her lips, and I turned away when I caught her staring at my face. "I disagree."

My breathing accelerated, and I could feel my pulse quicken. "Yeah? Well, you don't have a fucking clue what you're talking about. All the shrinks I've met do nothing but try to numb me on drugs. This one jackass told me that I should just get over my friend dying, treat his death like a bad breakup with a girlfriend. Fuck that dude. I have shrapnel from my buddy's skull embedded in my neck and my fucking psychiatrist thinks I should just get the fuck over it?"

She inched over to me on the sofa and placed a cautious hand on my thigh. I liked the way she touched me. She stroked my forearm, and I imagined her stroking my cock.

"Your therapist was clearly incompetent. But there are treatments that work," she said, her tone warm and soothing. "I just read a study that Transcendental Meditation really helps people with PTSD."

"Sounds like some quack hippy bullshit to me." I glared at her. "Fucking you was the best therapy I've had in months."

She bit her lip and removed her hand from my thigh.

"Hey, I'm sorry." Man, I shouldn't have said that. My grandma would whip my ass if she ever heard me talk to a girl like that. These days I'd lost my impulse control. The sooner Isa realized that I'd become a complete asshole, the sooner she would leave.

But I wanted her to stay.

"It's okay."

We finished our food in silence.

"So are you getting out of the Marines?"

"I don't want to, but I'm pretty fucked up, so I'll probably get forced out—it's for the best. I don't wanna be some fucking POG stuck at a desk, a twenty-year staff sergeant."

Her brow crinkled. "I don't understand. What's a POG? I thought you were a sergeant?"

I'd forgotten how to talk to civilians. "Person Other than Grunt. I am a sergeant. I meant that being a scout sniper was the only thing I ever wanted to do. I'd been selected for sniper course, but because I lost my eye, I'm ineligible. So I'm nothing but a grunt."

Grunt, that's who I was.

A warrior.

A motherfucking beast.

"Oh. Well, you can do anything now. You're a hero. Go to college, go on one of those cheesy reality shows, write a war memoir . . ." Her voice trailed off.

Fuck that. Why was everyone nagging me to go to college? I wasn't a dumbass, and I didn't need a goddam degree to prove that I was smart.

I hated reality television. My buddies gave their lives for our freedom and no one remembered their names. Yet these asshat celebrities posted selfies of themselves licking donuts and wearing American flags and were treated like gods.

As for writing a book, that sounded worse than therapy. I never wanted to be a public figure. The last thing I wanted to do was to have the details of my fucked up childhood exposed for the whole world to read.

"I'm not cut out for college because I can't remember shit with my brain injury. And actually, a producer asked me to be on that dumbass dance show —*Dancing under the Stars*. I guess every year they try to get some fucked up vet to compete, to balance out all the fame whores. I told him I'd rather go back to Iraq."

She closed her eyes for a second, a pained look on

her face. "Don't blame you. I hate that show. It's so fake."

Her tone sounded bitter, but it was refreshing to meet a girl who didn't seem to be obsessed with celebrities.

"And I've had several agents and writers hassling me about writing a book, but I can't write and I don't trust anyone with my story. So that's never going to happen."

Her mouth gaped, as if she wanted to say something else, but instead she just took another sip of her beer.

This sucked. I didn't want some chick telling me what to do, trying to inspire me. I yearned to take care of a woman, have her need me, not the other way around. "Why do you want to be a shrink? You must be pretty messed up—all the shrinks I've met had some serious issues."

She shifted in her seat and stared toward my balcony. "My mom died four years ago. I went through a really rough time, so studying psychology helped me."

Fuck, I was being a complete dick. I wasn't used to people being this open with me. Most girls just blew smoke up my ass. Even so, Isa clearly saw me as a project, someone to fix. Not as an equal. Not as a man. Definitely not as potentially her man.

"Sorry about your mom. My dad left before I was born, and then my mom abandoned me—I haven't seen her in years, though she must think I'm rich because she keeps trying to contact me ever since I got my medal. My grandparents raised me."

She nodded, and I could almost see her mind racing, creating some kind of psychological profile of me, pieced together from her knowledge of my actions that led to my Medal of Honor, the flashback she witnessed, my scarred face and body, and the brief tidbits I'd just offered.

Enough. This session was over.

I turned on the TV, landing on a channel airing the Country Music Awards. I didn't want to talk anymore, but I didn't want her to leave.

I never wanted to go out anymore—I'd become a recluse, holed up in my own world, alone with my demons. I'd only left tonight because I could go in costume, and look how that turned out.

Even so, I felt comfort in sharing our silence. After a few more songs, I knocked back my beer and knelt in front of her.

I lifted the T-shirt off of her body and just stared at her, sitting on my sofa in nothing but her black lace panties. Her cheeks were flushed; her breasts were soft and round, real. Her nipples looked like ripe cherries.

Her gaze focused on my face. She reached her hand out to touch my skin, and I recoiled.

"No, let me look at you," she whispered.

Fuck it; I wanted to get laid again, so I'd do whatever it took. If she wanted to examine me like some sort of circus side-stage attraction, I'd let her. Her soft fingertips traced my flesh, the charred remains of my ear, my scarred body.

"Can you see well? I mean, is your vision okay?"

"I see perfectly. I see your soft lips, I see your hard nipples, I see your trimmed pussy."

Her face turned pink. Guess she wasn't used to a man talking to her like that.

Enough of this bullshit. My hand grasped her neck, and our mouths met, my tongue probing her mouth. She made the sweetest little groan—less of a sigh, more like a purr. My cock became even harder, and my mouth focused on her nipples. I took one into my mouth, sucking, teasing, and my hand worked its way down her incredible body. Her belly was taut yet soft. I pressed on the fabric of her panties, her warm flesh slick with wetness.

A wicked smile graced her face, and she spread her legs wide, so fucking wide I was impressed. She was flexible as fuck. My mind filled with images, thousands of different positions I could fuck her in. I quenched that thought—this would probably be just another one-night stand.

But the night was not over yet. I rubbed her clit, and she writhed under my hand but kept her eyes focused on my face. Why? Why would she want to look at me? Did it get her off to examine my wounds? I didn't need a pity fuck. I flipped her on the sofa and pulled her panties off.

She gasped but pressed her ass backwards.

"Don't fucking move." I sprinted to retrieve another condom.

When I returned, she was in the same position— her curvaceous booty propped right up in the air. She gave me a coy glance over her shoulder.

I resumed my post, slapped her ass, and pumped my cock into her slick slit. Man, she felt incredible— wet, warm, tight as fuck. I kissed the back of her neck and rubbed her clit.

"Yes, ohmigod, Grady. Yes!"

I loved the way she said my name. My heart beat strong.

She let out a yelp as I drove deep inside her. I could fuck her for days. I could fuck her forever. But we might not have forever; as far as I knew we could only have tonight.

Her face flushed with pleasure. "Oh, baby, yes, just like that."

I loved a girl who knew what she wanted. This woman moved with the grace of a dancer as her hips swiveled around me, her pussy clenched and released my cock. I pumped her hard, my hand working her pussy, desperate for her climax. Desperate for my own, the only moment when I could experience pure joy and erase my pain. Forget for a few blissful seconds who I was and what I'd seen, what I'd done.

"Come for me, baby. Come all over my cock."

"Grady, oh, Grady. Yes!"

She exploded into moans, her pussy pulsating around my cock, the sensation pushing me over the edge. One deep groan and our physical connection, the moment we'd shared, was over.

I pulled out, gave her a pat on her ass, and walked over to the trash to throw the condom away.

I wanted her to sleep beside me, but I was afraid that I would scare her, wake her in the night with my screams, or even worse, choke her in my sleep. As much as I wanted to find someone to take care of, someone who could learn to love me, I couldn't risk endangering her.

And it went deeper than that. Even my closest friends weren't aware of all the dark stuff that existed in my mind. If Isa ever learned how clearly fucked up I was, she'd want nothing to do with me.

I wanted so much for a woman to truly see me—as a sexy man, as a protector, as her true love.

But I doubted I would ever allow myself to rely on a woman.

I'd had enough organs broken in my life; I didn't need a broken heart.

ISA

*O*kay, I was officially ashamed now. I'd slept with a man I'd just met twice in one night. This wasn't a date; this was a hookup. Exactly what I hadn't wanted.

And oh my God—how crazy random was this night? A producer asked Grady to be on *Dancing under the Stars*? What a nightmare. I could never tell Grady that I'd been on that show.

And even worse—he'd been approached about writing a book. I mean, of course he had, but I wondered if my father or his agent had asked Grady. I knew my dad had his sights on him. Dad kept waxing poetic about Grady's heroics. He'd even made a point to mention that he would love it if I dated a man like

Grady. Ha! If he only knew where I was now, I don't know if he'd be ashamed or thrilled.

Grady walked out of the bathroom, silent. I gathered my clothes and dressed. My costume barely fit with my sweaty body clinging to the fabric.

When I emerged, Grady sat on the sofa, blankly staring at the screen.

Okay. Awkward. "I'm going to go back to the party. It was nice meeting you." Isn't that what you were supposed to say after these hookups? How was I supposed to act? Was there any way I could turn this night around?

He stood up, and I admired his body again.

Stop it, Isa. He probably sees this as a one-time deal. He wanted to drive you home earlier and you insisted on staying. He hasn't mentioned seeing you again, asked what you like to do for fun, or shown any sign that this is more than just a hookup. Cut your losses and leave.

"I'll walk you back."

"You don't need to. It's just a block."

He grabbed his keys. "I said I'll walk you back. It's late; lots of guys have been drinking. A girl was assaulted on campus last week."

My belly fluttered—he was being protective over me, but it probably meant nothing. Was this some military honed instinct? He was a Medal of Honor recipient—I was sure this was just how he acted toward every woman. Whatever his reason, I enjoyed being the object of his concern. "Suit yourself." He probably wanted to head back to the party and find another Black Widow.

We left his apartment, the stars now shining over the San Diego night. We walked in silence to where Marisol had parked, but her car wasn't there.

Dammit.

I tried to think of a lie because I didn't want Grady to know I didn't have a ride. I didn't want him to feel guilt-tripped into driving me home. "My friend's car's gone. Let me text her real quick."

He grabbed my hand as it slid into my purse. "Gone? She left without texting you?"

I checked my phone. Yup. Nada. "Well, technically I left without telling her, though I did text her that I'd met someone. I'll call a cab."

He turned me to him. The starlight shone in his glass eye. "I don't trust cabs. Stay with me tonight, and I'll take you home tomorrow."

I couldn't get a read on him. Earlier he offered to drive me home; now he was telling me to spend the night. Did he really want me to stay or was he just worried about my safety? "Well, I trust cabs so I'm going to just call one."

"Stay." His grip tightened on my arm, but still I felt safe.

"Okay."

He put his arm around me and we walked back up to his apartment.

Now it was awkward.

He nodded, and then sat down, this time across from me. His gaze leveled me.

After a long swig of his beer, he finally spoke. "Where have I seen you before?"

Great. My insides quivered.

My gut wrenched as I thought about telling him the truth. If I had any hope of dating this man, this hero, I'd better not lie to him. After all, he'd been honest with me. But this situation was awkward enough. If I told him, I was sure he'd see me as some spoiled, rich reality star—the polar opposite of him being famous for saving his men's lives. But I wasn't spoiled or rich. I'd left that life. I wanted to help people who had gone through trauma. People like Grady, people like my mother.

People like me.

My hand rubbed my face. "Not sure, I guess I have a familiar face."

He shook his head. "No, it's not that. I may have only one eye, but I never forget a face. I've fucking *seen* you before. Don't lie to me." His voice was now gritty, rough, angry—a wave of fear flashed over me. I was alone in an apartment with a Marine with

PTSD. He was trained to kill. Hell, he probably *had* killed.

This was it. This was the moment, one of those pivotal moments I was certain I would agonize over for years to come. I could tell this man my truth in the hopes that we could turn this one-night stand into something more. But I knew from experience that the second he knew I had been on television, he would probably assume I was one of those trampy celebrity types who went home with everyone they met. Most men saw me only as a conquest once they learned about my past.

That fluttery feeling that I had had in my belly was now replaced by knots.

No, I couldn't allow a man I didn't know, didn't trust into a part of my life I'd said goodbye to forever.

"I'm not sure. Maybe you've seen me at another party or around town."

He exhaled, an audible sound of his disgust. He could probably tell I'd lied to him.

Great. I had just ruined this night.

After a few moments in silence, his phone rang. Saved by the bell.

"Hello? . . . Yeah, man, hold one sec." He looked at me. "It's my buddy, his wife just left him. Make yourself at home."

He opened the sliding glass door and stepped onto

the balcony, closing the door quickly behind him. I wanted to give him some privacy, so I grabbed my purse, headed into his bedroom, and went into the bathroom.

One look in the mirror, and I almost didn't recognize myself. My hair was wild, my eyes had mascara pooled under them, and my cheeks were splotchy.

I left the bathroom and something shiny caught my eye. His nightstand drawer was ajar, and a glimpse of steel deflected off the moonlight.

A gun.

A motherfucking gun.

My blood chilled. A flash of my mom's skull busted open, blood staining her gorgeous black hair, the smell of gunpowder, the lethal weapon still clutched in her hand, a final reminder that she'd given up the will to live. She'd never see me walk down the aisle; my future children would never know the love of their nana. After she'd taken her own life, I'd lost the desire to ever dance again.

My hand shook. Only an hour ago I'd seen Grady suffer from a combat flashback. He'd been blank, out of his mind, unreachable. What if he had another flashback and no one was around? What if this truly turned into nothing more than a one-night stand? Did he have someone to talk him down off the ledge? Would he call someone for help? I'd recently read an article about the suicide rates of vets and the lack of mental health care they receive. He'd even told me that he didn't believe any of the therapies worked. A grenade had blown Grady up. He'd watched his best friend die. Was he suicidal?

I peered out the window—he was still on the phone.

Luckily, I'd gone shooting with my dad many times prior to my mom's suicide, and I knew how to operate a weapon, though I hadn't seen a gun since I'd discovered her. My hand shaking, I slid the magazine out—it was empty. But I saw a single round in the chamber.

One round. One bullet.

Enough to end his life.

Enough to end mine.

I removed the round, clutched it in my hand, and buried the bullet in my purse.

I walked back into the living room, my heart racing, but I was certain I'd done the right thing.

But I was also certain I had to get the hell out of here. What if he found out I stole his bullet? In the haze of lust and desperation, I'd put myself in a dangerous situation—alone with an armed stranger. Emotions twisted inside me. Grady was sexy and a true hero.

But it didn't matter.

Ultimately, I didn't feel safe. Though I wanted to be a clinical psychologist, I didn't have the tools to help Grady, and one glance at the bullet in my purse made me realize I was in way over my head.

But what about our connection? I liked this guy— my heart raced when I thought about him. We had just had the most incredible sex, twice, and he'd opened up to me, revealed himself to me, showed me his scars. He asked me to spend the night. How could I leave him now when he had just begun to let me in?

After a few more minutes, Grady came back into the room. "Sorry about that, my buddy's going through a rough time."

"No worries. It's great that you're there for him."

We sat in silence. I didn't know what to say to him. I had so many questions about what had happened to him in Iraq, what his life was like now, how he coped. But I had no right to ask these questions. I never wanted to start a relationship with sex first. But we'd already crossed that line, and there was no going back.

My phone vibrated. Marisol.

Marisol: You hooker! You ready to go home?
Isa: I'll be back where you parked in a few minutes.
Marisol: K.

"Grady, my friend is going to pick me up downstairs. I'm going to go."

His face fell and it was as if I could almost see hope escaping from his eye.

What had I just done? I hated myself.

"Good." He stood up.

Good? Ouch. Maybe he had only asked me to stay the night because he was a gentleman. Guess he didn't want to be held responsible if a cabbie murdered me.

Or maybe the sting of my rejection had caused him to turn cold.

I'd been wrong to think there was a connection here; I was probably nothing more to him than another random hookup.

This was for the best. As much as I craved getting close to a man, I truly doubted that I could really let my guard down, especially with someone who was going through his own issues. Plus once he realized I'd disarmed him, he would probably never trust me again.

I refused to let him see my hurt. "It was really nice to meet you, Grady."

My arms extended for a hug but he brushed me off. Double ouch.

I wanted him to throw me over his back and take me back to his bed, fuck me all night. Grady's wounds, his scars of war, were likely so deep, that no amount of love could heal. Maybe he was actually right—no amount of therapy could help either, especially with an unwilling patient. He was not right for me—I couldn't risk getting involved with and loving another person who would leave me.

Pathetically I still hoped for a second that he would ask me for my number, or out on a date. Somewhere public, without a loaded gun in the vicinity. Some sign to show me that this was more than just a one-night stand.

But he just opened the door.

Isa, you're embarrassing yourself. He doesn't want anything to do with you. Just make a clean break now and forget this night ever happened.

I squeezed his hand, gave him a kiss on his cheek, and darted out of his apartment.

GRADY

*M*an, she couldn't leave fast enough, just like all the other girls. I'd been wrong, thinking there was a chance she could actually be interested in more than just a drive by. She definitely would never agree to attend the ball with me and be seen in public with a freak.

I threw my beer against the wall—shards of glass flying through the air, the liquid dripping down the wall.

Had I said something wrong? I didn't have a tolerance for bullshit or small talk. I never knew what to say to women. After living through the hell that was my life, talking about my favorite color or what movies I liked seemed so superficial.

This entire night had been so fake. Another meaningless hookup. I'd actually been about to ask her out before I had that flashback at the party. But once she'd followed me back to my place, of course I tried to fuck her. I'd hoped she'd stay the night, and maybe we could slowly learn about each other. If she'd seemed cool, I was going to ask her to the ball.

But asking her out was a dumbass idea anyway. I clearly couldn't handle being out in public, even with my face covered. Where could I take her? Some smoky bar where she wouldn't have to look at me?

I paced around my apartment, the blood pulsing violently through my body, my adrenaline spiking. Had she taken pity on me? Catnip to a wannabe psychologist? A pity fuck—that was all I was these days.

And I'd seen her before, but I just couldn't figure out where. When I asked her where, I could swear she was lying to me. My mind never cooperated anymore. Her face, her body, her eyes, even her voice. It was as if I *knew* her. But that wasn't possible. Maybe I was really losing it.

Fuck that bitch. It would've never worked out between us anyway. She was training to be a shrink. If I dated her, our relationship would turn into a never-ending counseling session.

Fuck women. I'd risked my life for my buddies and they had done the same for me. My love for my brothers was the only thing that mattered to me. My best friend was dead, and here I was acting like a pussy, stressing out because some girl I met took off. It didn't matter. None of this dating drama mattered.

Living in San Diego didn't help. I missed my hometown friends. And the Southern girls too. Everyone out here on the left coast only cared about appearances and money. I had neither.

I regretted ruining a perfectly good beer over this bitch. I grabbed another bottle, drowning myself in liquid regret. Each sip increasing my rage. Yes, I was a fucking alcoholic. And no, I didn't need any help.

I should've never left my place. I couldn't handle being around people anymore. From now on, I would hide away from the world. I'd fulfill my duties to the Corps and complete my required treatment.

I still needed to find a date to the ball, but it sure as hell wouldn't be Isa.

ISA

J woke up the next morning with the worst hangover, but it wasn't from the alcohol, it was from the guilt. My head throbbed, and my eyes were blurry. God, I hated myself for dashing out of there last night after he'd asked me to stay. I could've been honest with him about finding his loaded gun and asked him if he was suicidal. What was wrong with me? How could I claim to want to be a psychologist if I ran away at the first sign of trouble?

I also should've just opened up to him, told him I used to be on *Dancing under the Stars*. Maybe we could've connected. He would've probably understood how fame distorted reality since he was also in the public eye. A brief fantasy of grabbing brunch after incredible morning sex, maybe topped off by a walk on the beach later in the day, filled my head. We'd fall into a deep relationship before either of us really knew what had happened.

But more than likely, opening up would've just led to nothing.

But I didn't feel sorry for stealing his bullet. Granted, he was a Marine, so I was pretty sure he had more ammo around the house. At least if he had a weak moment, he would have to reload his gun, and even that short delay could potentially save his life. I'd missed all the signs that my mother was suicidal, so I refused to regret being proactive.

I did entertain the thought that my action could've possibly put his life in more danger. An intruder could break into his place, Grady could reach for his gun, think it was loaded, and then shoot, and lose his life. But that was the chance I'd taken, and my gut told me that he had a higher likelihood of committing suicide than of being robbed.

I Googled him the second I returned home. He had been so beautiful before he'd been injured. Kind of looked like a young Elvis Presley but with a way better body. I was still attracted to him, even with his disfigurement and scars. In a way, it made him sexier. More badass.

My fingers shook as I clicked away. I glanced around my room—a dust bunny perched on my nightstand, last night's costume in a pile on the floor, a day-old coffee mug on my desk. I definitely wasn't neat like Grady. I wondered if he had always been that clean and organized or if being a Marine made him that way.

I hoped he didn't think I'd left because of his injuries. I shuddered, thinking I could have possibly made him feel like he disgusted me. Maybe I was being conceited—he clearly knew he had a great body and could get any woman. Maybe he'd been relieved when I'd left.

Another link took me to his official webpage. I laughed when the page loaded—it played that song "Grenade" by Bruno Mars. I loved that Grady could keep a sense of humor about his injuries. On second thought, that song would make a good rumba . . .

I missed dancing, connecting to the floor, expressing the emotion of a song. For years it had been my outlet, kept me sane when my family life was chaotic. But after my mom killed herself during my last night on the show, the memories of me dancing had been laced with tragedy.

Wow, Grady wasn't the only one who needed therapy.

Despite all my intense work on myself, I was cognizant enough to realize that I was completely screwed up. I'd never been in a healthy relationship.

And my own interaction with my father was complicated. He'd become distant after my mom died, not that I blamed him.

And he refused to talk about my mother.

I tried to tell my father once how much I needed to share memories about her with him, but he claimed it was too painful to remember. I thought it was more painful to forget.

I closed my eyes, and replayed last night over again, haunting questions increasing my anxiety. Would I ever be able to find a man who was emotionally present and responsible? Would Grady ever recover from war? Could he move on from his traumas and find happiness in a normal, stable life? A man like that, so strong and sexy . . . I wondered what it would be like to be his.

But I'd never know. I'd closed that door before it was even cracked.

After stalking Grady, I finally closed the window, determined to push him out of my mind. I logged in again to my student services account, hoping the hold on my account had mysteriously vanished in the night, but unfortunately it remained.

Something was off. My father hadn't even returned my text.

A thought chilled me. Was he avoiding me?

I rummaged through my notebook to find my

passwords. Finally, I was able to log in to my trust fund, a fund I had set up with my earnings from *Dancing under the Stars*. I had made my father trustee.

The blinking screen seemed to take forever to refresh. But there was no mistaking the negative balance in glaring red.

-$359.

What in the world? This had to be a mistake. I had checked last quarter and had over thirty-five thousand dollars. Definitely more than enough for this final year of school.

I shot off a frantic text to my dad. Maybe he was in Vegas or on one of his benders? I would not wait for him to respond. First thing tomorrow morning, I would head to the bank. No one else had access to these funds— except my father.

And he would never touch it.

Would he?

GRADY

*M*y hand grasped the thin envelope, crumbling it in my fist. My heart knew the words written inside—*medically retired*. Not fit for duty.

Worthless.

I ripped open the letter, the stoic black ink confirming my worst fears. I was out, done. I'd be medically retired at the end of this enlistment—six more months. Nothing left of me but a broke-ass civilian, doomed to spend the rest of my life shuttered away from public view so I didn't scare the children. A future working the graveyard shift was my best bet so no one would have to look at my fucked up face.

Why hadn't I died in that shanty house? Honorably, a hero. Maggots eating my body in Arlington, a twenty-one-gun salute blazing.

At least I'd be with my best friend, Rafael.

I missed that motherfucker. His raw sense of humor, his supremely bad taste in music, his penchant for dousing his MREs in hot sauce. But more than anything, I missed the way he took care of everyone in our unit. He truly had our backs. If you needed some extra cash, Rafael wouldn't hesitate to lend it to you. If you needed a ride from the airport at two in the morning, Rafael would be there even if he were due to PT on base at six.

He had a wife and a beautiful little girl who worshipped him. Who missed him. Who would do anything to see him one last time.

I had no one.

No one would ever love me like that. No woman would ever want to look at me every day for the rest of her life.

It should've been me.

I jammed my key into my apartment, grabbed a bottle of whiskey, and blasted the death metal CD I'd left in the stereo.

San Diego was suffering from another late summer heat wave. The sun blazed outside the window, the excessive warmth incinerating my already torched skin.

I paced around my apartment, clutching my cell phone, but my fingers refused to press any numbers. I didn't want to burden my grandparents with my pain, my friends were in the field at CAX preparing to deploy to Afghanistan. I was jealous of those motherfuckers, training in the desert of 29 Palms, able-bodied, fearless, free. I was a prisoner of my body, my mind. Loneliness and despair crashed in a wave over me, drowning me in the agony I tried so hard to ignore.

I can't do this anymore.

Another swig of whiskey, and I knelt beside my bed. One shot, that's all it would take to end my suffering, my burden on this world. My spirit would soar free, leave my battered body.

Maybe it was my destiny. I shouldn't have survived.

I shouldn't be alive.

My life as I knew it was over. My career was finished. My best friend was dead. My body was in excruciating pain. I looked like a mutant.

No one would even notice if I was gone.

I grabbed my pistol, my Glock. No magazine; I always kept one round in the chamber. One click, and I'd meet my maker.

This wasn't the first time I'd thought about killing myself—I'd always kept my gun close by, in my nightstand, in my glove compartment. It was like a prescription that was always filled just in case I needed it.

It was time.

I wasn't afraid; I was at peace. I wanted to go home.

I placed the gun to my head, the cold steel imprinting on my temple, and squeezed the trigger.

Click.

Nothing. Radio silence.

What the fuck?

I was still here.

Fuck, I can't even kill myself.

Where the fuck was that round? I always left a round in my chamber.

Always.

No one had been in my apartment in a while. Only person who had been here recently was Isa.

Isa?

No way. No fucking way.

But it could only be her. No one had broken into my place to steal my bullet.

How did she know how to disarm a weapon? When had she done this? While I was in the shower? On the phone with my buddy?

I placed the gun down, debating going into my

closet to get more ammo. But I just sat still on the bed, frozen.

I couldn't believe that bitch had stolen my bullet. What if I needed my gun to protect myself?

If I ever saw her again, I'd make her pay. But I didn't even know how to contact her. No last name, no phone number. Nothing. Only a memory remained that replayed daily in my mind. The sensation of her hot, wet flesh, of how being inside her erased my pain, if only for a fleeting moment.

I buried my face in my hands. And for the first time since my injuries, I allowed myself to cry.

One tear burned my skin, and it was like I had opened up a floodgate. I wept for Rafael, I wept for myself, and I drowned myself in self-pity. What had I ever done to deserve this fate? I was caught in an endless cycle of surgeries, intolerable pain, agony, and no relief.

I grabbed my bottle of whisky and downed it, the smooth liquid coating my throat, taking the edge off my aching. The framed picture of the President awarding me the medal came into my view, and my breath hitched. I was not worthy of such an accolade —the highest military honor in the country.

After staring at my gun, I stood up and placed it back in my nightstand. Once again, I'd cheated death.

I would make no promise for tomorrow, but tonight would not be my end.

ISA

*M*y hand shook, my coffee spilling through its tiny plastic slit. This bank opened at nine in the morning, and I'd been standing outside for the last half an hour. Worry gnawed through me. This was more than money—this was my life, my future, the only lasting benefit of my past.

The teller finally opened the door at a minute past nine. I marched to the back of the bank and sat in the manager's chair.

A middle-aged man with a glint in his eyes and an ill-fitting suit greeted me. "Good morning, Miss. How can I help you?"

I handed him my driver's license and bankcard. "There's a mistake in my account. My tuition check bounced. I looked online last night and it said there was a negative balance. That can't be correct. I had over thirty-five thousand dollars in it a few months ago."

He glanced at my ID. "I see. Please swipe your card in the reader and enter your PIN, and we will get to the bottom of this."

I followed his directions and pulled my hair.

The manager gave me a sympathetic grin and perused his screen. After the annoying tapping of his old-school keyboard, he nodded his head toward me.

"I'm sorry to say that unfortunately your balance is in the negative. It seems a transfer of funds was made into another account last month."

"No, that's not possible. This is my college fund. I don't ever transfer out of it."

He turned the screen towards me. My eyes registered what I was seeing, and I could feel my heart drop. "It seems the other owner of the account went into a branch in Temecula and transferred the money to a personal checking in his name."

Temecula.

My hometown.

My temples throbbed with rage.

"I see. I'm sorry for the inconvenience." I stuffed my cards in my purse, grabbed my coffee, and dashed out of the bank, praying I would reach my car before tears welled in my eyes.

My father had stolen my money.

All of it.

No wonder he was avoiding my calls.

I slammed the car door and hunched over the steering wheel. I knew my dad was an alcoholic and hadn't written anything worth publishing in years. But to steal from his own daughter?

I turned my keys in the ignition and pressed on the gas pedal.

My father would not get away with this. He better pay me back every damn penny, or I'd have him arrested.

But no matter what I had to do, I'd find the money to graduate.

GRADY

*A*nother fucking waiting room. Man, I was
sick to death of doctors. Probing my flesh,
their compassionate yet condescending smirks, insincere offers of hope. Today, I'd get another skin graft,
fuck my life.

I shifted in my seat, wishing I were anywhere but
here. This place was stuck in the eighties, like I was
on a *Miami Vice* set: Kenny Loggins played over the
speakers, the walls were painted pale peach, the air
reeked of baby powder and bleach, and a vase of
plastic flowers was placed on the floor, not even
worthy of a cheap coffee table.

I pulled out my phone but had no fucking recep-
tion. Dammit. My hand shuffled through the basket

of magazines; a *Playboy* would've been nice, but I'd settle for a *Men's Health*.

I grabbed a pile of crap—last year's *Good House-keeping, Star, Vogue*. I was about to give up and just stare at the cracked paint when something caught my eye.

A "Ten Years of *Dancing under the Stars*" special edition. And there in the corner of the cover was a small picture of a girl dancing. Black hair, incredible body, killer smile.

Isa.

The hot chick from the one-night stand I couldn't stop thinking about, the girl who stole my bullet.

What the fuck?

I focused on her face, her body, her hair. It was fucking her. I'd bet my medal on it.

I knew I'd seen her before. I'd even fucking asked her why she looked familiar but she lied to me. Couldn't for the life of her know where I could've possibly seen her? How about fifteen million people watched you every night for two years? My grandma loved that show—used to force me to watch it every fucking week. And now I remembered that Meemaw's favorite dancer was "that sweet American girl."

I thumbed through the magazine, desperate for some more intel.

Bella Applebaum won the 5ᵗʰ and 6ᵗʰ seasons of Dancing under the Stars. She left the show in the middle of the 7ᵗʰ season, with no explanation. Her current whereabouts remain unknown.

Isa. . .bella?

Why did she leave the show? Unknown whereabouts? Why the secrecy? What was she hiding from?

A reality star—of course she'd never want a relationship with me. She'd probably run off and marry some liberal war-protesting Hollywood pretty boy.

She was like one of these goddamn celebrities who pretended to support our troops but actually charged the charities to make appearances. Give back to your country, fuck a war vet.

My mind raced. Who the fuck did she think she was, trying to disarm me? I needed to see her again— get some kind of closure. I'd fucking flat out ask her why she slept with me, then ran the fuck out the door the first chance she got.

Man, I sounded like a bitch. I just couldn't accept that I'd read her so wrong. I honest to God thought she was into me. The sex was incredible, and she hadn't abandoned me after my PTSD freak-out at the party. She seemed to want to get to know me even if it was only to help me since she claimed to want to become a psychologist.

And that damn bullet. Maybe the episode at the

party had been tolerable to her, piqued her psychobabble curiosity, but once she found herself trapped in an apartment with a PTSD war vet with a loaded gun, she bolted. I can't honestly say I blamed her. I was a fucking mess.

"Mr. Williams, we're ready for you now."

I glanced up. A hot young nurse waited to escort me back to a room so I could be tortured. My flesh would be manipulated and scraped so I could pass for a human and not an alien. A swig of the whiskey hidden in my water bottle took the edge of my pain.

Across the room, I recognized a fellow Marine, his leg amputated, his wife clutching his arm, attempting to comfort him. I wondered what it would be like to have someone like that in my life who would love me no matter what.

I stood up and followed the sexy nurse down the barren hallway. Meeting Isa, having her take my bullet, seeing her in the magazine, these incidents couldn't all be coincidences.

I had to see her again.

ISA

I sped on the freeway and drove an hour and a half north to confront my father in Temecula.

Normally, I loved going home, but not today when my anxiety was burning through my body. How could he take my college money—money I had earned on my own? And why? Was it a gambling debt? I'd worked so hard to graduate on time. The mere thought of having my entire future destroyed because I'd trusted my father was unbearable.

Our home was nothing extravagant, just a simple three-bedroom, two-bath, ranch house. But there was comfort knowing I could return to the place where I'd taken my first steps, spent merry Christmases, and had learned how to dance from my mom.

My hometown wasn't well-known—it had a few vineyards, and a bunch of motocross racers and UFC fighters lived there. But it had a strong community network—it was a place Ronald Reagan made famous by praising its hardworking citizens for rallying together to build a sports park.

As I pulled on our street, I noticed that our grass was unusually brown and patchy—more than was even normal in this drought. The trim on the door was faded, and the annuals I had planted in spring had already wilted. Even so, our bright pink crape myrtle was in full bloom and the lone avocado tree was bearing fruit.

I grabbed my bag, and as I headed up the drive-way, my dad greeted me at the door. He wore his classic uniform of a wrinkly flannel shirt and worn jeans, and his strong, woodsy cologne mixed with his alcohol-spiked breath quickly hit my nostrils. His face was unshaven and his salt-and-pepper hair was unkempt. I winced—I hated seeing him so broken. In my memories, my father had always been strong, proud, and attractive. I knew he blamed himself for my mom's suicide, no matter how many times I told him there was nothing we could've done.

He quickly surveyed my face. "Don't give me that look; I'm fine."

Every muscle in my body tensed. I followed him inside the house.

"You look wrecked. Why did you take my money?"

He paused, his eyes pained.

I knew that look.

"Now, Dad. Spill it."

He remained silent. I forced myself to remain calm and not blow up at him. I headed into the kitchen to start the coffeemaker. Bills were piled near the telephone, and a few boxes were packed against the wall —as if he was planning on fleeing. "Did you read an organizing book or something?"

"No." He gazed out the window at the peek-a-boo vineyard view.

"Why are your things packed?"

"Just doing some cleaning."

I leveled him with my eyes.

He let out a sigh. "Okay. You got me."

Fuck. I knew that tone.

"What's going on with you? Where the hell is my money? The truth, please."

Beads of sweat pooled on his neck.

"I'm bankrupt. I hadn't paid the property taxes and was behind on our mortgage so I used the money to catch up. The bank was going to foreclose on our home."

I clenched my fist, and my vision became cloudy.

"How on earth are you bankrupt? You had a six-figure advance for your last book. Didn't you invest?"

"That book deal was five years ago. The critics loved it but it was no bestseller. I earned out my advance and that was that. I need a hit."

I poured coffee into two mugs, debated emptying the pot on my father's hand. My dad by no means lived an extravagant lifestyle. We had always lived within a budget, which was probably why it was easy for me to adjust back to being a starving college student after my brief time as a starlet.

But my house, our home, meant the world to me. It was more than a roof over our heads. I could still hear my mother's voice echo down the hallway, I could still picture her tending to the garden, I could still inhale the scent of her perfumed clothes.

He continued his excuses as I struggled to remain calm.

"I've approached everyone I can think of to write a biography, but either they're already working with a writer, or my agent doesn't think we could get a big enough advance from a publisher." His voice was choked with emotion but I refused to pity him.

My mind immediately flashed to Grady. If he wrote a war memoir, it would be a bestseller. He'd told me he had no desire to write one, but I wondered if he would ever change his mind.

"So you stole from your own daughter? I need that money for tuition. I won't graduate. It's my money. How fucking dare you? I can have you arrested."

"I know, I'm sorry. My agent assured me that this celebrity would choose me to write his book, so I thought I could take the money out of the trust and deposit it back before you ever noticed. It was wrong of me and I don't blame you if you hate me, but I didn't want to tell you. I'll figure this out, I promise."

I was not reassured. Rage flashed through me. "Can't you sell the house and move somewhere else? That'll buy you some time until you find your next subject." The second the words left my lips, hollowness filled my core. My home. The place I'd escaped to when my face had been plastered on every tabloid in America, the community that had embraced me when everyone else turned their back on me.

"Even if I sell the home it won't help. I'm underwater on the mortgage, and I'd need to find a new place to live. I have three months of expenses left with the money I took from you, and then I have nothing."

Memories rushed back of picnicking with my parents at the duck pond, exploring the candy and root beer shops in quaint Old Town. My childhood had been happy—I'd never had a clue that my mom was in such private pain. And my parents always seemed so in love. I had dreamt of having my own happy marriage one day—but now that image was shattered. My mom wasn't content—she was miserable. If I had read her so wrong, how could I trust anyone?

"How much do you owe?"

He started speaking rapidly. "Maybe it's best if we lose the home. Who knows how long I'll be around anyway?"

"Is that supposed to be comforting? How much debt do you have?"

"Forty-seven thousand dollars."

Forty-seven thousand dollars? We were screwed. Royally screwed. I could never come up with that kind of money, unless I went back on *Dancing under the Stars* for a season. And that was completely out of the question. I hadn't danced in years and was completely out of practice. There had to be another way.

"I don't want to lose this house, Dad. We have so many wonderful memories here. Do you remember the time that Mom found that white bunny in our backyard? Our neighbor wanted to feed it to the coyotes. But Mom nursed him back to health. She loved little Latte."

My dad's eyes narrowed and a vein popped in his neck. "I hated that rabbit—another one of your mom's projects that she started but then abandoned when she lost interest. I ended up taking care of that thing."

I slammed my coffee mug down. "Why do you do that? Every time I mention her, you either dismiss me or get enraged. We had good times, happy times. Why can't we talk about her?"

"Because she left us! Suicide is selfish. She didn't care about or love us or she wouldn't've done it!"

I raised my hand and slapped him, the tight sting of my palm shocking me. "How dare you! She was not selfish. She was sick! How can you not see that? She did love us—she probably thought we were better off!" I was completely stunned by how ignorant people were about suicide. I admit I'd thought the same things my father just said, that she didn't love us, that she was selfish. Thank God I'd educated myself. I just wished my father would try to understand. Try to forgive.

My father didn't say anything to me. He didn't need to. He exhaled and his hand started shaking.

"I'm sorry. I shouldn't have slapped you."

"It's okay, I probably deserved it. I just miss her."

And that was the first time my dad admitted to me that he missed her.

I didn't know what to say. The intersection of anger, hurt, and resentment brewed inside me. "Why didn't you tell me about the house sooner? Can't you take another job? Anything?"

"You don't think I've applied for everything? No one wants to hire a middle-aged man. I just need a chance and I can turn this around. Just one more hit."

Could I dare ask Grady? He would say no, and he didn't seem to want anything to do with me. He hadn't even asked for my number. What was I going to do? Stop by his apartment?

Maybe I could contact him through Facebook, though he didn't even have a searchable profile, just a page.

No, I couldn't do that. I didn't even know Grady. And I'd ran out on him.

There was one other person I could ask.

"Don't worry, Dad. It'll work out. I'll pray for a miracle."

He exhaled and his eyes looked up. He hugged me. "Thank you. I'm really sorry I took your money."

I racked my brain. I could apply for a school loan. Or take a one-quarter leave to figure this out. But one thing was certain—I could only rely on myself.

.

GRADY

*A*ll fucking day I couldn't get Isa out of my mind. How she'd sucked my cock, the image of her ass as I took her from behind, the expression on her face when I licked her pussy, the sweet sounds of her moans as she came.

Remembering how it felt to be inside her numbed my pain. The throbbing from my skin graft was intense, like being dragged around on a carpet until my skin melted off.

I sat down to my computer and Googled her.

Bella Applebaum—Dancing under the Stars.

Her face lit up my screen—hair darker, skin tanner, and body skinnier. I thought she looked way hotter when I'd met her than she had on the show—I liked my women with curves.

She'd danced two seasons, then left mid-season. No reason why. She'd obviously changed her life—instead of dancing with losers she now was sleeping with monsters.

A few pics with her ex-partner—Pasha, a fellow dancer on the show. I wonder if he ever fucked her? Looked like a pansy. I mean, the guy fucking waxed his chest.

I scanned a few more articles on the screen, until one headline sent a jolt through my body.

Inside Bella's private hell: the truth about the night when the reality star discovered her mother's body.

I skimmed the article—though Bella had never confirmed the story to the press, the rumor was her mom had been shot by an unknown killer.

Fuck.

Maybe that's why she stole my bullet . . . she'd been scared I would harm her.

And little did she know I'd be dead if it weren't for her.

My head buzzed and a devious thought passed through my head. What if . . . I accepted the show's offer? Agreed to make a jackass out of myself—as long as I was allowed to choose my partner.

The producer had called me again last week. Said he'd do "anything" to get me on the show.

Anything.

And honestly, what the fuck else was I doing with my life, besides drinking myself into oblivion? To be honest, I needed a plan B. Now that I was about to be retired from the Marines, I'd be left at the mercy of the VA, waiting two years to get an appointment. I had no formal education, no ability to hold down a job with my injuries, no future.

The producer had offered me $125,000 to do the show, plus a weekly bonus if I didn't get eliminated. I could make up to a half million dollars. The Corps would definitely give me leave—anything for public relations. That was who I was these days anyway. A fucking propaganda puppet.

If the public wanted a war hero, I would give them exactly what they craved.

I relaxed back in my chair and entertained the possibilities. The dancers were forced to train their partners up to eight hours a day. I could demand that she was my partner.

It was a fifteen-week season.

Fifteen weeks to fuck Isa.

Fifteen weeks to make her need me. Show her the kind of man I was.

My hand picked up my phone but my fingers refused to dial the numbers.

No. I couldn't do it.

I wouldn't do it.

And it wasn't because I thought it was gay or lame or anything like that. There had been other war heroes who'd starred on it, and my staff sergeant, Bret Lord, had been on as a professional dancer on the show, and he was masculine as fuck. He'd donated his entire salary to his buddy's widow.

But he wasn't fucked up like I was.

It wasn't even the ridiculous outfits I'd have to wear or the makeup they'd paint on my face.

It was the triggers.

They would be everywhere. Flashing lights, sound stages, the audience clapping.

I'd snap. I'd break. I'd humiliate myself. I thrived on routine—one of the only suggestions my therapist had made that I actually implemented. Get up, go to the hospital for forced therapy and medical appointments, return home, get drunk, get laid.

But I hadn't been with anyone since Isa. She'd been different than the other girls I'd fucked. I wanted to claim her as mine.

I was almost crazy enough to embarrass myself on national television to find a way back to her.

Almost.

But that was a stupid fucking idea. For so many reasons. The most important being that if I had fifteen weeks alone with Isa, I'd become addicted to her. And then she'd leave me.

As a Medal of Honor recipient, I was held to a higher standard. I would not humiliate the Corps. And having a flashback on national television would be unavoidable.

Then again, blowing my brains out would've clearly brought shame to the Marines, but at least the publicity might've shed some light on the suicide rates of veterans. What the fuck was wrong with me to even be thinking that? Man, I needed help.

I ripped up the producer's number and threw the card into the trash.

Maybe someday Isa and I would cross paths again, and I'd be able to show her the kind of man I was.

A beast.

ISA

*a*fter a silent breakfast, where I spent most of my time internally debating whether or not I should contact Grady, my father turned on the television and found a football game. Once he was distracted, I told my dad I had some errands to run.

I needed to talk to Benny Brooks, the executive producer of *Dancing under the Stars*.

I jumped in my car and headed to the freeway, but I didn't have the guts to show up on Grady's doorstep —instead I was going back to LA.

I hadn't been back to Hollywood since my mom killed herself not wanting to be in the city where she'd taken her life. But I was desperate now. I had to finish school. I'd do whatever it took. And this option was infinitely preferable to making an ass out of myself groveling to Grady.

And the truth was, I missed dancing.

My foot pressed on the gas pedal. It was Monday in the middle of summer. *Dancing under the Stars* was not filming nor was the show on tour. And it was only three weeks until United States Dancesport Championships—which meant all the dancers should be training. I no longer had Benny's phone number and no one ever answered the studio phone, but he was usually coaching Pasha at his ballroom.

I checked Pasha's Instagram. At least he was there —he had endorsed a workout shake from the ballroom less than an hour ago.

Two hours, an iced coffee, and a caramel apple empanada later, I parked in the studio's parking lot. This studio had been my home for many years. I'd done rumba walks until my toenails popped off, jive kicks until my knees gave out, and samba rolls until my back ached. But no matter how much physical pain I'd endured, I'd enjoyed every second of it.

My mouth became dry. I exited the car and placed my hand on the door. Before I could change my mind, I forced myself to walk inside.

But the second I stepped into the studio, I immediately regretted it. I didn't belong here—I was an outsider, a quitter.

Pasha whirled around the floor with his new professional partner, a stunning Russian blonde who also just happened to be his new girlfriend. I couldn't help but stare at her toes, the effortless way they rolled off the ground.

A bunch of younger dancers practiced their cha cha locks in the mirror. Luckily, no one had noticed me. I contemplated dashing back to my car, but a familiar voice stopped me.

"Bellichka?" Pasha had ditched his partner in the middle of the floor and walked over to me.

Bellichka, Pasha's pet name for me. "Privet, Pasha."

The man who stood before me hadn't aged a day since the last time I'd seen him four years ago. Pasha's blonde hair was slicked with gel, his eyes were a pale blue, and his body was lean and tan. I was pretty sure that his flawless skin was the result of Botox.

I expected him to hug me or at least give me one of those fake kisses on the cheek. But instead, his gaze traveled my body. I felt naked in his presence. He'd never looked at me like that, ever. All the years we danced together he'd treated me like his little sister. I had yearned for him to want me, see me as a woman and not as a little girl. I'd been so jealous of his girl-friends.

But now, when I looked at him, I felt nothing.

He took me in his arms and hugged me,

attempting to kiss me on the lips, but I turned my cheek. He seemed startled and quickly released me.

"What it is you doing here?"

Well, his accent was still strong, despite being on television. "I was looking for Benny."

"He is not here. He went to Australia to take care of something."

Dammit. There went my plan.

"But I can help you. . ."

Doubtful. But I hadn't come all this way to give up so easily.

Pasha said something in Russian to his partner, who had come over to investigate. Years of immersing myself in Pasha's language and culture allowed me to loosely decipher what he had said. "Go practice. It won't be long. She isn't of your concern."

Ouch. Well, it was true. I hated the way he talked to her, the way he had talked to me. But he wasn't my problem anymore.

He took me to the office and I sat down on the loveseat in the corner. There were old pictures of us hung on the walls, a trophy in a case behind a desk. "Why you come to Benny?"

"I was wondering . . . my dad has run into some trouble, and the truth is I'm tight on cash. Do you think he could get me back on *Dancing under the Stars*?" I cringed with shame the second the request left my lips. Here I sat, in my jean shorts and T-shirt, begging my ex-partner to help me out. I'd left the show and our partnership. Why would he ever help me?

"I wish I could help with you on show, but I cannot. Do you need the money? How much it is that you need, I write you check." He reached into his desk drawer and pulled out a checkbook.

"No, no, I don't want your money. I want to work."

"Work? Let me be honest together with you. You will not get back on show." He stood up from the desk and joined me on the loveseat. His hand pushed a lock of hair out of my face and I resisted the urge to recoil. "You are now beautiful to me. What we had, I will never have again. Oksana, she is incredible dancer, but you, Bellichka, when you danced, you were like magic."

I steadied my breath. "Okay. Then if I'm so incredible, why can't I get on the show? Aren't you a co-producer now? You can help me."

He laughed. "I am not head producer of show. Benny is. And he wants young dancers, more young than you. You are now twenty-three. The waitlist it is long. Unless celebrity requests to you, you will not be picked." He inched into my dance space, and this time, I retreated. "But you can come back to me, work at studio, compete together with me, I can take care of you, like you always wanted. If you work very hard, we can win again."

What? Was he serious? I didn't want to date him now. Back then, I'd idolized him and that life. But now, I saw it as shallow. We had devoted our lives to dancing, not ever thinking about anyone other than ourselves. After meeting Grady, a man that had sacrificed so much for something he believed in, I wanted to be with someone inspiring. Someone who inspired me to be a better person.

"That is a kind offer, Pash, but I'm not interested. Nice to see you again. Good luck at Nationals." I stood up, and he mirrored me. I turned to leave, and he pulled me to him, kissing me on the cheek. But I felt nothing. Once there had been electricity between us, but the spark had extinguished. Until I met Grady, I'd wondered if I would ever feel that radiance from a man again.

I wanted to feel that heat again.

By the time I returned home, my father was passed out on the sofa. I crept by him and went to my room.

My bedroom was stuck in time, high school blaring from every corner. Trophies and pictures from my dance competitions adorned the walls, pictures of me winning Nationals with Pasha.

My stomach fluttered, and I opened my laptop. Now I had an excuse to contact Grady.

But it wasn't even a good excuse. *Hey, I know I ran off after we had sex, but will you let my alcoholic dad, who stole my tuition funds, write your war memoir so I can pay for college?* I'd be just another one of the people in his life who wanted to use him.

But it was more than that. I couldn't stop thinking about him. I had to see him again. Even if he just laughed in my face.

The worst he could say was no or ignore me. But maybe, just maybe, we could reconnect.

I moved the cursor over to the message tab on his page. "Grady Williams: Public Figure." It even had one of those blue checkmarks next to his name so I knew it was legit.

Did he even manage his own page? Maybe I would send him a message and some assistant would respond? I was sure he received hundreds of emails daily from women in love with him.

I scrolled down his page. Mostly motivational quotes, very few pictures. One of him sharing a beer with the President outside the Oval Office, another one of him with his battalion before the grenade. And a final picture of him and his buddy off-roading. I stared at that last picture longer than I should have. The inscription read "R.I.P. Rafael."

Damn, I'd learned from reading reports of his

attack that Rafael was Grady's friend who died next to Grady.

I clicked the message button, my heart palpitating, and started typing.

Isa: Hi Grady. I was wondering if we could meet for coffee.

Once I hit Send, my insides begin to quiver. Then I saw that check mark. Grady had read my message, or someone maintaining his page had. Grady was typing.

Grady: Come by my place tomorrow night at ten.

Whoa. He didn't even ask me when I was free, or where I wanted to meet. Going to a man's place at ten at night was definitely a booty call. Maybe he thought I wanted another round. I'd be lying if I said I didn't crave him. Though I'd contacted him, he was in control of the situation. I didn't know if I should be turned on or pissed off.

Isa: Okay. I'll be there.

I sat in my bedroom, my stomach fluttering. What had I just done? A few days ago I'd been a sexually frustrated college coed eager to finish school. Now unless I could come up with tuition, I'd end up being a college dropout who couldn't stop thinking about her epic one-night stand with Grady the sex god. I kept replaying every moment of our night in my head. The way he touched me, the way he made me feel, the way he focused on my pleasure.

But now I had a second chance to see if there was something more between us than just red-hot chemistry, to apologize for running off, to figure out if I had been wrong about being scared of him.

GRADY

*T*ime had passed slowly since I'd received Isa's message yesterday. I was driving myself crazy trying to figure out why she'd contacted me, secretly hoping that she wanted another round. Ever since learning about her mother's death, I'd been almost certain that she'd taken my bullet because she was concerned. I was excited for another chance with her.

After a quick workout, I took a hot shower and dabbed on some cologne. The steam from the shower cleared from my mirror, and I caught a glimpse of my face.

I would never get used to my reflection. The droopy eye, the non-existent ear, the skin that looked like it had been slashed by a serial killer. A lump grew in my throat, and I closed my eye.

I threw on a black T-shirt and some cargo shorts and paced around my place.

A chime rang out—Isa was downstairs. Adrenaline rushed through my body, the same feeling I had when I stepped out on the battlefield.

I buzzed her in and stood by the door.

Before I saw her, I heard her steps. Heels for sure, delicate little taps coming down the hallway. Her scent filled the air—fresh, fruity, fascinating.

Damn, she was beautiful.

She wore one of those loose T-shirts and tight skinny jeans that showed off her juicy ass. Her hair cascaded past her shoulders, and I wanted to run my fingers through it while she screamed my name.

"Hey, beautiful." I pulled her to me and gave her a hug, my cock pressing against her crotch.

"Hey. It's good to see you. How are you?" Her voice was cautious yet soothing.

"Good." I didn't have any tolerance for small talk. I wanted to know why she wrote me. I wanted to know exactly why she ran out the other night. I wanted to know why she stole my bullet.

After I released her, she headed to the sofa. My mind flashed to remembering her perfect naked ass perched up as I took her from behind.

She rubbed her hands down her jeans and every inch of me desired her.

I stared at her chest. "Do you want a drink?"

"No, I'm good." She ran her tongue over her teeth, and her gaze darted across the room.

My gut gnarled. Something was up. She wasn't making eye contact with me, and I suspected that it wasn't just because of my face. "What's up?"

"I just wanted to see you."

Nice non-answer. "Well, now you've seen me."

She pulled on her hair. "Well, I don't want you to think I only came over here to ask you for a favor."

A favor? I clenched my fists. My heart felt like it was literally shrinking. Of course she wanted something from me—these days everyone did. A woman that beautiful could never be interested in dating a man as grotesque as me. I hated myself for believing for a second that I had a chance with her. For believing that if someone could fall in love with me, then maybe I could love myself.

She pursed her lips. "Are you okay?"

"I'm fine." What did this bitch want? I nodded toward her. "What do you want?"

Her hands kept twirling her hair. "Can we talk first?"

I shot her an irritated glance. "Talk about what?

We aren't friends. We just fucked once. What the fuck do you *want* from me?"

The color drained from her face and she shook her head at me. "My father, he's a bestselling biographer. He's really talented, a complete perfectionist, and like I already told you, he's a Marine. I was wondering . . . if there was any way you would consider letting him write your war memoir?"

Yup, the bitch was no different than the other women I'd met since I'd been injured. I was a novelty, a charity, a commodity. God, and I honestly believed for a second she wanted me. "The answer is no. Why don't you get the fuck out of here? You're just like every other fake-ass bitch I've met, *Bella*. And you washed up reality stars are the worst—using anyone to stay relevant."

Her chin trembled. "Bella? I guess you found out I was on *Dancing under the Stars?*"

"Yes, ma'am. I may only have one eye, but I told you that I'd seen you before. I never forget a face."

"I . . . I'm sorry. I didn't want to tell you because once I tell a guy about the show, he treats me differently. I like you, Grady, I honest to God do. But I figured if I told you I'd been on a television show, you'd judge me, like you're doing right now. That show destroyed my life. That's why I quit. I wasn't asked to leave, I ran away."

Just like she had that night. Her lip trembled and I knew there was more to her story for leaving. But I was too pissed to keep interrogating her. "You saw my gun, didn't you? Did you take my bullet?"

Her face turned white. "I . . . I mean—"

"I'll take that as a yes. Why? Did you think I was going to kill you? Who the fuck do you think you are? I'm a Marine. This is America. I have a right to have a loaded gun in my house without some bitch stealing my goddamn bullet." Here I was yelling at this girl, my body bursting with rage when she'd saved my life. She probably thought I was a psycho. I just wanted her to leave.

But instead of cowering, she glared right at me. "I didn't know you—I still don't. I saw you have a flashback at that party, and yes, I thought it was a possibility that you could be violent or even suicidal. So yes, I did take it, and no, I'm not sorry. And you know what? I'd do it again!"

Whoa. As pissed off as I was at her, I was impressed that she was standing up to me. No one ever told me off anymore. Even my own friends pussyfooted around me ever since I was awarded my medal.

My eye darted around her face. She seemed sincere, hurt, even scared. Whatever, it was too late now to even try to turn this around.

I lowered my voice. "It's fine. I don't want to write a book, but thanks for asking. And if I did, I could pick any author I wanted. I definitely wouldn't pick the father of some random girl I fucked. It's time for you to go."

But the bitch kept talking, her voice laced with desperation. "No, wait. Listen to me—my dad's an excellent writer. He will do a great job. I know you don't want to tell your story, but if you don't, I'm sure someone will write an unauthorized account of the attack. This is your way of controlling the information, honoring your friend's memory."

She had a point. I'd already read some bullshit accounts in the press. Most were exaggerated, made me look like I was lying. Yes, I threw myself on a grenade—no, I wasn't the bionic man who withstood gunfire and killed a bunch of people.

I studied Isa—her chest heaved as she talked and I spied a pink bra strap. My rage began to melt away, replaced by lust.

I wanted her. Again. However I could have her.

"Why is this so important to you? If your dad is such a great writer, he can write some other guy's story. Why mine?"

She cast a downward glance. "He's having some financial trouble now. The bank will foreclose on our home, and—" she sighed, "well, he stole my tuition money to try to save the house. It was my money I had earned when I was on the show. So, yeah, I won't be able to finish my last year of college unless I can come up with the cash."

What a fucking dick. What kind of dad does that? "I'm not going to trust my story with some jackass who steals from his daughter."

"No, wait. He's not a jerk, I swear. He's desperate. He's been a mess since my mom died. And he was in Vietnam so he has his own PTSD issues. He's an alcoholic and he has flashbacks too. But I know he'd do an amazing job. I promise you that he's a brilliant writer. He was even nominated for the Pulitzer. And honestly, he's so in awe of you. He first told me about your story before you won your medal. He thinks you're a hero. You *are* a hero."

My mind raced. She was desperate.

And I held the power.

So now I'd get what I wanted.

"What's in it for me?"

Her eyes brightened. "My dad's agent is excellent. I'm sure you'll get a huge book deal."

I laughed, leaned in closer, and eye-fucked her slowly. "No, that's not what I meant, baby. I'm not talking about the money. If I agree to do this, and choose your father, what are *you* going to do for me?"

ALANA ALBERTSON

"Oh." Her face finally registered the meaning behind my question. "What do you want?"

"I want you to be my date for the Commandant's Marine Corps Ball. I'm the Guest of Honor. We'll fly to Hawaii together, spend a weekend attending official events, and when the weekend is over, we will go our separate ways."

"Wow." Her lips widened into a smile. "Grady, I'd be honored to be your date to the ball. When is it?"

"November tenth. The Marine Corps Birthday."

She beamed. "That's a few months away. I can't wait. Yes, of course."

I let out a laugh. No way was I going to let her off that easily.

"Don't get too excited. There's more to the deal. I want the full girlfriend experience."

Her smile dropped. "Full girlfriend experience?"

"Yup. I need you to pretend to be my girlfriend in public, at the ball, and at any events we have to attend. The President will be there. I can't exactly bring my fuck buddy to meet the leader of the free world. One year, the guest of honor tried to bring a porn star to the ball and the commandant banned him. The tabloids have interviewed my ex-girlfriends, so I really want to keep this clean and avoid a scandal."

"Makes sense. I understand."

"No, you don't understand. In order to pull this

126

off, we need to get to know each other. I want you to myself. No drama. Just you and me, alone, away from the rest of world. Whatever I say goes. You disobey me, and I won't sign the contract with your father. Once the ball is over, we go our separate ways." I moved toward her, placing my hand on her upper thigh. "But until then, I own you. All night, every night. On your knees sucking my cock, on all fours while I fuck you from behind. I want to lick your pussy until you're begging me for release. I want to fuck you until you can't do anything but come and come and come for me."

Her skin flushed, her eyes blinked, and her lips parted. I couldn't tell if she wanted to slap me or kiss me. "Sorry, I'm not for sale. This was a mistake. I'm going to go."

I laughed and grabbed her wrist. "You're not going anywhere. You contacted me; you asked me for a favor. Look me in the eye and tell me you don't want me again."

She swallowed hard and I remembered how hot she looked sucking me off. "Our night together was incredible, but it was a mistake. I'm not looking for a fling. I can't have sex with you every night and not get attached. I know you must think I'm a slut, but you're the only man I've ever had a one-night stand with."

I'd heard that line from many girls—but some-

ALANA ALBERTSON

thing in her voice made me actually believe her. "I
don't think you're a slut. I think you're a good girl
who wants to get wild, who wants to be tempted and
cut loose. Use me, Isa. I'm not your fairy tale prince,
I'm your beast."

Now she rubbed her hand over her heart, her
mouth alternating between gaping open and closing
shut. "I . . . I don't know what to say."

I pulled her into me, tilted her head toward my
mouth, whispering into her lips. "Say yes and I'll
make all your fantasies come true." My lips kissed her
neck, and my hands gripped her wrist. I flipped her
under me, and she writhed against my body. This kiss
was urgent, menacing, yet at the same time comforting. My tongue explored her hot little mouth, until
she let out a little whimper.

"And you swear you'll let my dad write your
memoir?" She kissed me back, her leg wrapping
around my waist.

"I give you my word." I pinched her nipples, and
took off her shirt.

"When do we start?" she asked breathlessly, her
hands exploring my body, tugging at my shorts.

"Now. Get on your knees and suck my cock."

Her hand undid my belt buckle, and my pants
dropped to the floor. She pulled down my black boxer
briefs, releasing my cock from its prison.

Her soft lips brushed against my tip, and the anticipation was almost too much to handle. How many nights since I'd met her had I jerked off thinking about her doing this exact thing? In my fantasies, despite myself, I imagined her as mine. No labels, not my girlfriend or my wife, but mine—all mine. No other man would ever feel her lips on his cock—she was only for me.

Her hand grasped the base of my cock and slid up the length. She licked her lips, teasing me, and I was desperate to feel that tongue on my tip. I resisted the urge to place my hand on the back of her neck and guide her to me. She knew what I wanted—and she was about to give it to me.

She kissed the lower part of my stomach, licking her way down my happy trail, clearly enjoying that she literally had me in the palm of her hand. I'd do just about anything for her right now. After what seemed like an eternity, she finally took me deep, her hot, little mouth creating a tight ring around my cock. She sucked me so hard I could barely handle the pleasure. I wanted to fuck her mouth, pound the back of her throat, but I didn't want to scare her. One glimpse of my primal desire, the beast within, and she could leave me again.

"Fuck, baby, that feels so good."

She pulled out all the stops—her hands gliding up

and down, her lips pressed against me, her tongue darting under the base of my tip.

I gripped her hair, trying to push her off me.

"I'm going to come. Stop."

But she didn't stop. She kept sucking, licking, and stroking. I closed my eyes and allowed myself to let go, and a wave of complete ecstasy reached every cell in my body. Isa didn't recoil in disgust; she lapped up my cum like a kitten devouring warm milk.

I pulled up my boxers and shorts and clutched her to my chest. I debated asking her to stay but I had to check into my unit tomorrow to start processing my exit paperwork

"I'm traveling to Lake Tahoe; I have a cabin for a week. I want you to stay with me."

She nodded. "Okay, when?"

"Next weekend. I'll message you the details." I took out my phone, and we exchanged numbers.

"Okay, that works. Grady, I . . . I wanted to apologize for running—"

I stopped her. "We're not going to do that." Though I wanted to know the reason she'd bolted, I didn't want her to lie to me. And I couldn't trust her to tell me the truth. We had a week together to get to know each other. Telling her I wanted nothing to do with her at the end of our deal gave us both an out.

"Oh, okay. Bye then." She squirmed away from me. I walked her to her car, and watched her drive away.

The traffic buzzed, triggering my anxiety, and I needed to get back inside my place ASAP before I lost it. What the fuck had I just committed to? A book? All because I couldn't get her pussy off my brain?

At least I had a date for the ball. I just hoped my bargain wouldn't blow up in my face.

I reasoned with myself that all the decisions I'd made were good decisions, decisions for my future.

I did want to tell my story, to honor Rafael. And I would refuse to do any book signings. Give the public the patriotic war story they craved, and then retreat back into my shell.

And getting to fuck Isa for a week in exchange was the best book bonus I could ever receive.

ISA

I drove alongside the ocean to meet Marisol for coffee. I hadn't told her yet about my deal with Grady because I didn't want to deal with her negativity. She would no doubt be apprehensive about me heading to some mystery cabin with some dangerous Marine I barely knew. I also couldn't risk details of my agreement with Grady being leaked to the press. I refused to do anything to jeopardize my dad's book deal. But I needed to confide in someone, and despite her tendency to gossip, I did trust her.

I sat at Bird Rock Coffee in La Jolla, people-watching through my dark sunglasses. Young mothers dressed in their Lululemon leggings strolled by pushing their kids in BOB strollers. Businessmen dressed in surf clothes and Reef sandals held meetings on their laptops.

When I'd left Grady's place and the fog of lust disappeared, I was livid. How dare he demand sex in exchange for letting my dad write his book? But I'd since calmed down and attempted to see it from his perspective. We'd hooked up, I'd stolen his bullet and left. When I'd finally contacted him, it was to ask for a favor. I secretly hoped his demands would be for more than just sex, that he wanted to get to know me. I guess I would know soon enough.

Marisol finally showed up, fifteen minutes late as usual. We hugged and took our place in line to order our lattes. Since there was nowhere to sit at the café, we took our drinks down to Calumet Park, a little area that overlooked the ocean and sat on a small cement bench.

I sipped my drink, the nutty macadamia flavor transporting me back to Hawaii. Last time I'd been on the island was for a *Dancing under the Stars* tour, only months before my mother died. And now, I'd be attending the ball there with Grady.

"So, girl, what's up? What's so urgent?"

"Not much, just studying for the GRE. You?"

She sipped her beverage. "Oh, just spending time with Paloma and working at my dad's restaurant trying to save up money."

Marisol definitely liked to have a good time, but that girl worked harder than anyone I'd ever met. She didn't even learn English until she was six years old, and she graduated top of her class in high school. In order to pay for college and medical school, she'd joined the Navy ROTC program. A year later, she found out she was pregnant. After she graduated from undergrad and medical school, she would serve in the Navy.

"Did I ever tell you how cool I think you are to join the Navy?"

She gave me the side eye. "Is this about Grady again? Are you still thinking about him?"

She knew me too well. "Yes, actually it is. I saw him again. Well, I wrote him first. And I'm going to visit him in Tahoe next weekend."

Her eyes widened and her long lashes blinked. "You're kidding me. Why did you write him?"

Marisol knew everything about my mom, my father, and me. I could tell her what was really going on. "The truth is my dad is in debt, going to lose our house." I paused. "Don't tell anyone, but he stole my tuition money trying to stop the bank from fore-closing."

"He stole from you? Damn, chica. I know he's your dad, but that's straight fucked up."

"I know. I'm pissed. But it's in the past—getting

mad isn't going to bring the money back. What could I do? Press charges?"

"Uh, yeah. He should figure this out, not you. Why do you have to always clean up everyone's messes?"

Good question. "That's not the point. I don't want to lose the house either."

"Fine, but what does this have to do with going to Lake Tahoe with Grady? Oh my God! Did you hook up with him again?"

"Uh. . .yeah. I can't help myself when I'm around him. He's so sexy—like electric. I actually asked Grady to let my dad write his memoir. He said yes—if I went to Lake Tahoe and the ball with him."

Marisol grabbed my shoulder. "And you agreed? Are you nuts? Are you forgetting the fact that this dude had a flashback at the party, threw you to the ground, and then you found a loaded gun at his house? I've been around some of these PTSD vets at the VA, and some of them are nuts."

She had excellent points.

"I've thought this out. I even admitted to him that I stole his bullet. But here's the thing—I can't stop thinking about him."

A toddler boy played with his dog in the grass. I smiled at him, hoping his nanny hadn't overheard our conversation. She seemed to be staring at me but maybe I was just being paranoid.

"I call bullshit, Isa. I don't care how amazingly he fucked you, and believe me, I'm no saint. And I'm not judging you. But he's dangerous. He's unstable. He's a recluse. So you go away with him, he fucks your brains out, you go to the ball with him, and your dad writes his book. Then what? You pretend you never met him? You're playing with fire."

"It's more than that. I like him; he's fascinating. I mean, what kind of guy throws himself on a grenade?"

"A crazy one. Dude's got a death wish. If I saw a grenade, I'd run away."

"Right. That's the thing. He was willing to die to save his friends. He has to be a good man, just messed up."

Mirasol pursed her lips. "I guess. And let's be real . . . his scars don't bother you at all?"

I gulped. "I mean, yeah, his scars are horrific. But it doesn't matter. He's still incredibly sexy."

She downed the rest of her latte like it was a shot. "I know you admire him. But—and I don't mean to be a bitch, honey—he's not your mom. You can't save him. After all the crap you've been through with your mom, you can't be in a situation like that again. It wouldn't be healthy. From what you told me, Grady needs help. Real help. I'm not saying that you guys could never find common ground, but I just don't want you in danger."

I turned my head away from her and stared out to the ocean, fixating on a rock with a bunch of brown pelicans perched on it. Marisol was right. I'd fought so hard to overcome my depression and fear, to stop blaming myself for not realizing my mom was hurting. But my healing came from within. Grady needed to find a way to live with his injuries and his memories. Playing house with him wouldn't solve anything.

GRADY

$\mathcal{M}$y buddies threw me a "going to fuck a reality star" party. I couldn't believe Isa had actually agreed to my demands. As a show of good faith, I'd exchanged a few emails with her father and his agent. Her father was incredibly excited and passionate about the project, and I felt confident that he would completely dedicate himself and write an honest, heartfelt memoir. His agent was certain he could sell the memoir at auction for six figures—apparently the American public was hungry for "heroic tales of valor." I embraced the idea of writing the book once I realized that I would be able to tell my story my way, without embellishing it. But I refused to sign the contract with the agent until after my vacation with Isa, just to make sure she kept her promise to me.

Some patriotic Silicon Valley multimillionaire I'd met at a fundraising function had offered to let me use his mansion, his vacation home, whenever I needed to get away. He owned a waterfront house in Incline Village that he pretty much never used. I'd initially told him there was no way I could accept his offer, but he'd said it was his honor to lend his home to a hero. I still felt uncomfortable being praised, but I thought some time to detox would do me some good. Better yet, a free house to fuck Isa in wasn't the worst idea in the world. My favorite type of therapy.

Beau, Diego, Trace, and Preston all took leave for a few days to party with me in Tahoe before Isa arrived. These men were my brothers—we'd all fought together, we were the survivors of the attack.

Beau raised a bottle of Sierra Nevada Celebration Ale. "Here's to the best Devil Dawg I know. Get some!"

We all drank, and the other men milled around the cabin. This place was sick. Had its own sandy beach, a hot tub on the deck, nestled in the pines. Maybe I could find some peace out here, besides losing myself in Isa's pussy.

Diego smirked, his eyes reflecting on the lake

behind him. "Man, I can't believe you fucked Isa. She's fucking gorgeous."

"Yup. But she's just another stuck-up celeb. She's only agreeing to spend time with me if I let her dad write my memoir. I'm not doing the book for her, I'm doing it to tell my story and honor Rafael. And the money is nice. Maybe I can buy a place out here so I have somewhere to go since the Corps finally decided to kick my broke ass out."

Trace placed his hand on my shoulder and I brushed it off. I was jealous of this motherfucker. Before my injury, the two of us would hit the clubs, compete to gain the attention of the hottest girl in the bar. There was no competition now—he'd win every time. He had everything going for him. He rocked his boy-band smile, was in perfect shape, had just completed sniper school, and had escaped our attack unscathed. He had a future in the Corps, for as long as he wanted it.

"Whatever, dude. The Corps medically retiring you is a good thing—groups will pay you to speak, politicians will milk your Medal of Honor for all it's worth."

I sighed. "But I don't want that—I hate public speaking. I don't want anyone pitying me. I want to go back overseas. I want to fight. I want some action."

Trace again put his hand on my shoulder, and this

time I didn't remove it. "You're looking at this all wrong. Write your book, rake in the cash, fuck your hottie girl, get out of the Corps, and you can do whatever you want. Hell, go on *Dancing under the Stars* and every chick in America will want to fuck you."

"Fuck that. You go on. You'd look good in the makeup and shit."

"Whatever, man. I'm telling you. You've got it made."

Easy for him to say—he still had his looks, his career. The career that should've been mine.

All my friends were living their dreams. Diego was going to McMap to be a Marine Martial Arts instructor, and Beau was going to become a Marine Security Guard at the Embassy. We were young Devil Dawgs—raised on Eminem and Facebook. Most of us had never even thought about life after the Corps. Do twenty years, retire, get a paycheck for life. If we were lucky, find a beautiful girl who wouldn't fuck around on us while we were deployed.

Trace had the balls to look me in the eye. "And, dude, no one pities you—they admire the fuck out of you. You saved my life, bro. I'd be dead without you. And I know you think any of us would've done the same thing—but you're wrong. You're the man."

I shrugged him off of me. The world looked different to me now. I needed to navigate my new

THE BEAUTY AND THE BEAST

reality—find a career or job I could feel as passionate about. I believed everything happened for a reason— my injury, getting offered to write this book, meeting Isa. I had to figure out why God had allowed me to live.

ISA

*T*he wait was over; my time alone with Grady would start today.

I'd flown into Reno this morning and spent the past hour driving my rental car to Lake Tahoe. He'd offered to pick me up at the airport, but I insisted on renting a car. I didn't want to be completely dependent on him just in case anything went wrong.

Even so, he would be in control.

In other words, he would be my master.

As I approached Incline Village, I marveled at the beauty of the Emerald Bay. I rolled down the window —the scent of freshly fallen pine needles mixed with the mountain air tickled my nostrils. I needed this retreat. A time to relax, read some books, finish that Christmas needlepoint stocking I'd been working on for years—I could definitely think of worse ways to spend the week, especially since I was still unable to enroll for fall quarter. I'd applied for a loan, but because I'd missed the deadline, I wouldn't be able to attend.

But there was nothing I could do about that now. All I could hope for was that this week with Grady would go smoothly, that we would have a great time at the ball, and that he would keep his promise and let my dad write his book.

And maybe, something deeper would develop with Grady.

I followed the navigation system and pulled in front of a towering log cabin with a view of the lake.

I took a deep breath, steadied my nerves, and walked to the magnificent door. It was gorgeous— hand-carved mahogany featuring a bear eating honey from a tree.

I pressed the doorbell, and Grady opened the door. His muscles bulged out of his T-shirt but seeing his scars in the light sent a shock through my core. I gasped, in spite of myself.

Grady's fingers pressed deeper into my flesh, and I let out a yelp.

"You're mine now, baby. And this time you can't run away. You're going to be forced to look at me every day." His voice was urgent and dripping with sex.

His eye shot a dagger at me and then he finally released me.

I gulped.

I'd hurt him.

He must've thought the only reason I wanted to see him was to ask him to do the memoir.

But that wasn't true. As much as Grady scared me, I was drawn to him.

Before I could speak, he'd turned and disappeared into the cabin, slamming the carved wooden bear door behind him.

I didn't know whether I should be flattered or scared or pissed off.

The only thing I did know was the heat of his body next to mine had made me ache to be with him again.

GRADY

*A*ll I had wanted was to spend some time with her, and I'd promised myself I would try to start fresh. But seeing her outside, looking so damn sexy, triggered rage inside me. Rage that she would never be mine, rage that she was only here because I'd forced her hand, rage that she was only agreeing to be around me so she'd have enough money to finish school. I wanted her to choose to stay with me because she wanted me, not because she felt being fucked by me was the only way to save her father's ass after he stole her money.

My solitude was short-lived. Isa cautiously opened the door and headed to the sofa. Her scent filled the room—she smelled like whipped cream and strawberries.

She was wearing a tight-fitting yellow sweat suit and flip-flops with rhinestones. Despite her incredible body and heart-shaped face, she didn't look fake or hard like a few of the celebrities and models I had met. Her smile was very genuine, and I had yet to see her in heavy makeup.

We were alone together. Truly alone.

I sat on the distressed leather sofa and just stared at the lake. My ears pounded and I cracked my knuckles.

If she wanted to, she could talk.

It only took her a few minutes.

"Can we talk? I really want to start this weekend off in a good place."

"Shoot."

"Okay. I want you to know that I'm not just here because of the deal with my dad. I want to be here. I want to get to know you."

I didn't believe her. Words were cheap. She would have to show me that she truly wanted to spend time with me. It would probably help if I stopped being such a dick.

"And the only reason I left after we hooked up that night was because I panicked," she said.

"Panicked about what? I thought you left because you thought I was suicidal. Did you think I was going to hurt you?"

The color drained from her face, but she made strong eye contact. "For a second, yes, I believed it was possible. I mean, you had a loaded gun, were drinking, had a flashback. But not just that. I didn't really see hope for anything beyond one night with you. I'm attracted to you. You have the best body I've ever seen, you're incredible in bed, and I don't mind your scars. Honestly, I don't—they actually make you sexy. But you told me you didn't believe in therapy. Neither did my mom. I'm not a psychologist, and I don't know you that well, but I really think you need to find some type of therapy that works."

So I had actually been wrong about her; she hadn't wanted to save me; she'd wanted nothing to do with me. And she saw me as someone who couldn't even take care of myself.

Though she'd saved my life by taking that bullet, I'd never admit my moment of weakness to her. Once I told her I'd attempted suicide, she'd probably bolt again.

I tried another approach.

"Look, I've tried every medicine I've been given, every talk therapy. Honest to God, nothing has worked. But I'm open. I don't want to live like this."

Her face seemed to shine. "That makes me happy."

My promise to attempt more therapy seemed to soften Isa. Her shoulders relaxed and she moved closer to me on the sofa. I put my arm around her and pulled her into me. This was more like it.

"How did you find out I was on *Dancing under the Stars?*"

"I saw your picture in a magazine at my doctor's office. Well, *Bella's* picture, but I'd recognize you anywhere. But I think it's cool. I'd love to see you dance."

She shook her head. "I'll dance with you at the ball, but I doubt I'll ever compete again or dance like that."

"Why'd you quit?"

She stared distantly toward the lake. "After my mom died, it was too painful. She was a dancer. Every time I stepped on the floor, I'd remember her teaching me, I'd search for her in the audience. I needed to figure out who I was without dancing, without her, without my partner."

She paused on the word "partner." Had that douche been her boyfriend? The thought of that slimy motherfucker touching Isa made me want to break his skinny legs. At least she wasn't still dancing. I would never tell a woman to quit her passion, but I was certain I couldn't handle watching another man grope my woman, wrap his hands around her waist, stroke her thighs. I'd seen that show, the tiny costumes she wore, the seductive dances they did—I'd be too consumed with jealousy to have anyone I was dating be on it.

"And the book? You feel okay with writing about what happened?"

"Yup. You were right. I want to tell my story, my way. And I need the money. I'm pretty fucked up, physically and mentally. I have to prepare for my future, especially since I'm about to get kicked out of the Corps."

Her eyes opened wide. "I'm sorry, Grady. I had no idea. You'll find a new career to make you happy."

My head bobbed forward. She didn't know shit about what made me happy. I was a warrior—that was the only thing that had mattered in my life.

"So, I've emailed your dad a few times and talked to him on the phone. He seems pretty cool—for a thief."

"Ha." She hesitated. "He's okay. He's going through a rough time—he really needs this break, so thank you again. Don't worry—he'll do a great job on your memoir."

I winced. A father should protect and provide for his daughter, and here Isa was the one taking care of her dad, a man who'd stolen from her. But their fucked up relationship wasn't my problem. At least she had a parent in her life. "I won't tell him. This is the only thing I'm good for now—telling heroic war stories. Instead of shooting guns, I'm being wheeled out like a Smithsonian exhibit to make politicians feel guilty about the war and to open their wallets up."

Her chin dipped down. "I'm sorry. I never meant to make you feel like I'm just another person who is using you. Maybe this was a stupid idea—I should've never asked you. Maybe we should just forget this whole idea. I feel like such a bitch."

Damn, did this girl always try to run at the first sign of trouble?

Her chest heaved, and I decided to stop being such an asshole. I wanted her however I could have her. I was going to give this relationship, or whatever it was, everything I had.

I moved closer to her and put my arm around her. "Stay, but it's your choice. I'm not going to force you. I'm not going to hurt you. You're safe here with me. I'd be lying if I said I hadn't thought about our night— how you screamed my name, how sweet you taste."

"I want to . . . I just think we moved too fast. I'd like to take some time, move slowly. Let our emotional connection catch up with our physical connection."

I hopped off the couch and stood in front of her, our bodies inches from touching. "We've already slept together, baby. And I plan to fuck you every night for as long as you're here. In fact, I'm gonna fuck you now." I pulled her to me, needing to feel the heat of her body. "You can't deny how hot we were together. Look me in the eye and tell me you haven't dreamt of me, that your body doesn't miss my touch, that you don't ache for me."

She looked down at her toes. "I—I want to, but I'm scared. It's complicated. Once a picture of us gets out in the press, everything will change, you'll see. We're both in the public eye. People will make up stories about us. We'll be in the tabloids. Fans, people, think they know us. They think they own you."

"I own you." I cupped her face and kissed her, and a shot of heat rose to my cock.

She kissed me back, deep, passionate kisses, kisses that assured me that she wanted me as much as I wanted her.

I ran my hands through her hair. "Tell me what you want, baby."

"You, I want you. All of you."

I controlled my breathing, wanting to take my time with her, not rush. I picked her up and placed her on the long oak coffee table.

I unzipped her sweat suit, and removed her tank top. I had never seen anything sexier than her yellow lace bra with a red bow in the middle of her ample cleavage.

I licked at her nipples through the fabric, sucking

and tugging slowly until she moaned. I unhooked her bra, freeing her breasts.

She spread her legs and I slipped my arm around her waist, pulling down her pants. Matching yellow lace panties—it truly was my lucky night.

"Talk to me baby, what do you need from me?"

I could tease her all night. I dusted her with kisses, making her come alive with my mouth. I licked her thighs, around the lace border of her panties, pressing my lips to her heat, desperate to taste her.

"I—I want your tongue."

Yes, ma'am. I hooked the edge of her panties and removed them. My tongue moved, licking her lips, savoring her taste. The image of her rubbing her nipples, her body reacting to my mouth was almost enough to make me come right then.

I pulled a condom out of my pocket and quickly undressed. She stood up and I rolled the condom over my cock, sitting down on the sofa. "Straddle me."

She flipped her hair out of her face and climbed on my lap, slowly guiding my cock inside of her. She gasped when I slammed her deep.

I kissed her neck, buried my head into her chest and sucked on her nipples, my other hand squeezing her amazing ass. She rode me, controlling the rhythm, tossing her head back, rubbing her clit against me. The reflection on her incredible body in the window, knowing that someone could be watching us, made the moment even hotter.

"That's it, baby. You're so fucking beautiful."

Her pace quickened, and I was dying to make her come harder than she ever had before. I rubbed her clit, licking her nipples, until I knew she was close, so fucking close.

"Oh, Grady, oh, baby."

She let out a deep moan and I could feel her pussy clench. I let myself go also, the intensity of my own orgasm shocking me.

She climbed off of me and I went to the bathroom to throw away the condom.

When I returned, she'd put back on her clothes.

"Where am I sleeping tonight?"

I quickly dressed. I wasn't ready for her to sleep next to me. I didn't want to scare her with my night terrors. "In the guest room. Get your rest. You'll need it. I'm going to get your things."

I went out to her car, grabbed her bags, and returned to Isa.

I led her to the spare bedroom.

Her eyes opened wide. "This place is beautiful. Thank you for inviting me."

She gave me a hug and I held her tightly.

"You can go anywhere except up to the third floor where I sleep, unless I invite you. I don't sleep much, but if I'm lucky enough to crash, I don't want to be awakened. If you need me, just press the intercom, and I'll come downstairs."

"Okay. Good night."

I gave her a sweet kiss, the first kiss we'd shared that didn't lead to sex. Then I held her tighter than I'd ever held anyone. Why did she feel so good when nothing in my life was right? Why did I want her so badly? Could she really be the one woman who could make me feel like a man again?

"Isa, I'm really glad you're here."

ISA

J exhaled, relieved that Grady and I had been able to have a good talk. Just the switch that I was now here by choice, not under coercion, alleviated my anxiety. I wanted to be here. Grady wanted me here. We were both going to explore if we had more than just a physical connection.

My room was as nice as any hotel room I'd ever stayed in when I was competing. It had a stone fireplace, a huge spa tub, and a king-sized wooden bed covered with a bear-patterned quilt.

I drew myself a hot bath and slipped into the soothing water. My breath quickened when I reminded myself that I was naked in the same house with Grady. Maybe there were cameras in this place and he was watching me. That thought excited me— my chest heaved as I imagined Grady finding me naked in the tub, his strong hands exploring every inch of my body. Being around Grady brought out all my fantasies.

Once the water turned cold, I quickly dressed in my pajamas and relaxed in the bed, excited for the next day. My nerves eventually calmed down . . . until I heard a scream in the middle of the night.

Well, at least I thought it had been a scream. I sat up in my bed, startled, breathless, but eventually realized it probably had been a nightmare and fell back asleep.

The scent of bacon wafted through my bedroom and roused me from what had actually been the best sleep I'd had recently, despite being awakened by the noise in the dark. For once, I didn't wake a few times during the night to worry about paying my tuition, didn't have to sleep with the windows open because my dorm didn't have air conditioning, nor did I have to drown out the noise from the freeway that ran parallel to my place. Instead, the sound of birds chirping, the warmth of the fire, and the peace of knowing that there was a chance I'd still be able to graduate swept me into a blissful dreamland.

I headed into the bathroom, wondering if Grady was waiting for me. After washing my face, and brushing my teeth, I examined my outfit, which consisted of a tank top and fuzzy pajama bottoms. For a second I had an urge to flee, giving in to my anxiety, but I instead opened the door.

Ay dios mío!

The sight of Grady cooking breakfast made me drool. He wore gray sweatpants and a tight, long-sleeved thermal shirt that hugged his muscular body.

"Good morning, sexy," he called out.

"Morning." The sunlight beamed through a skylight and I took the time to study the cabin. A huge staircase led upstairs to a loft area, a gourmet kitchen beckoned me, and a beautiful stone fireplace warmed the room. I was mesmerized by the view of the lake. This place had to be worth at least a million dollars.

"Please sit down. Would you like water or orange juice?"

I sat at the breakfast table in front of an already awaiting coffee mug. "Water would be great, thank you."

I watched him walk in the kitchen and noticed a slight limp that I hadn't seen before. I tried not to stare, but my mind refused to quiet with all the questions I had.

He emerged from the kitchen carrying a glass of water and a dozen red roses.

Swoon.

He placed the glass of water down, leaned into me, and handed me the roses.

"These are for you."

My belly quivered, pleasantly surprised by the sweet gesture. I inhaled the scent of the roses. "You're so sweet. Thanks for the roses. They're beautiful."

"Not as beautiful as you."

My heart fluttered.

"Are you hungry?"

I nodded. He returned to the kitchen and plated an omelet, bacon, and fresh fruit. Coffee was awaiting me at the table. I'd been single since I'd left the show, and I couldn't remember the last time someone had taken care of me.

It was hard for me to accept.

"You really didn't have to do this. I can cook for you if you like. Maybe I can go grocery shopping later today? I make killer chicken enchiladas."

"Let's relax today. How did you sleep?"

"Great. It's so peaceful here."

I took a sip of my coffee and tasted the omelet. I detected a hint of goat cheese and some fresh herbs. It was delicious. "So, have you decided what you're going to do when you get out?"

"No."

"After the book comes out, I'm sure you'll be asked to do interviews. I can give you some media tips."

He squinted his eye. "Not interested. I'm going to tell my story once and then vanish until I decide what I want to do with my life. I don't want to be that guy who spends the rest of his life capitalizing on this one event."

"Right, I get that, but people just want to hear your story. It's so inspiring."

"Look, I see you staring at my hand and my eyeball. I'm clearly fucked up—but I'm sick to death of talking about it. Ever since it happened, that incident has been my entire life. Every person I meet fixates on my injuries and the circumstances surrounding them. Before I was maimed, I was just a normal man. I want to be him again. The minute anyone sees me, or finds out who I am, they treat me differently. Everyone does. You do."

Wow. That was kind of deep.

"Okay. I understand. But I don't treat you differently because of how you look—I treat you differently because of what you did. But I do get what you're saying. When I was dancing, everyone expected me to look and act a certain way. Sometimes I just wanted to be a normal girl."

"Exactly." His gaze focused on my chest and I realized I wasn't wearing a bra.

"So, I know we discussed this last night, but I want to be clear of your expectations. We're just getting to know each other?"

I anxiously awaited his response, hoping I was reading this situation correctly. "I still have the ball to go to in November. You'll pretend to be my girlfriend for the event. But I'll be honest with you, Isa—you're insanely hot, and you seem sweet, but I'm not looking for a serious relationship until I can figure out my life. It wouldn't be fair to you."

A tingling swept across my face, and I couldn't help faking a smile to mask my disappointment in his answer.

"Got it. Me too, I mean with the serious relationship thing. I want to focus on graduating from college. So what does pretending to be your girlfriend entail, besides the incredible sex?"

He laughed, reached over the table, and grabbed my hand, his deep red scars contrasting with my pale skin. "I'm a man, you're hot, of course I want to fuck you every chance I get. But I need our arrangement to be drama-free."

Damn. Well, glad we cleared that up. But I had to admit, the intensity in his voice, the strength in his hand, the delicious way he said *fuck*, made every part of me ache for him.

"Good to know. I assume I'll meet some of your friends before the ball so we can pull this off?"

His lips curled, but since half of his face was covered in scars, I couldn't tell if he was amused or annoyed. "You assume correctly. Any more questions or can I finish my fucking breakfast?"

Definitely annoyed. I flinched. I'd clearly pushed too hard. "Of course. Sorry for the interrogation."

We ate in silence. As I savored each bite, I wondered what the ball would be like. There had been a time in my life that I'd spent dressing up, going to ballroom competitions, enjoying meeting new people. But I hadn't been that person in years.

He stood up from his chair, his hand trembling, his face now pale. "I don't feel well. I'm going to go up to my room."

"Are you okay? Do you need to go to the doctor?"

"I'm fine."

"Okay, what should I do?"

He leveled me with his eye. "Read a book." His voice was gruff, unsettled, and tinged with anger.

I finished my breakfast quickly and retreated to my room. Well, Mr. Nice Guy bearing flowers hadn't lasted long. I was probably already annoying him. But I felt better knowing his intentions. To be a respectable girlfriend for hire. We clearly had to get to know each other to pull the charade off.

ALANA ALBERTSON

That night Grady grilled burgers, still not allowing me to cook for him. He pounded beers all night, and we barely spoke a word. The tension hung thick in the air. Yes, we'd had sex, incredible sex, but we didn't know each other at all. Basically, I was holed away in a cabin with a stranger. The full scenario was simultaneously nerve wracking and unbelievably hot.

I was also struggling to understand his reactions toward me. He probably couldn't stand me and was regretting inviting me as much as I was second guessing coming here.

He retired to his room with a curt goodnight, didn't even try to get intimate with me. I felt so undesirable, but I had to remind myself that I was the one who asked him to take it slowly.

I also felt useless. I'd never just sat around. I wanted to clean the house, organize something, be productive. Instead, I went down to the basement, sat on the sofa, and turned on the television.

A scream roused me from my sleep. This time I was absolutely certain it was a scream, not a nightmare. I must've crashed watching the movie. Dammit. I woke up shivering, forgetting for a second where I was.

I ran upstairs, worried that maybe there was an intruder, or Grady had been hurt. The main floor was eerily quiet. The hair on my arm stood up, and I made the decision to go against his orders and creep upstairs to the third floor. When I reached his room, the door was shut. I debated knocking, but before I could make a decision, I heard another groan.

What was going on in there? I knew that groan—it was the sound my mother had made when she was in agony, when her migraines were so intense that she was sobbing in pain.

My chest stuttered, so I listened by the door, praying not to get caught. After a few seconds of silence, another moan—deep, guttural, haunting. Definitely not of the sexual variety—it was as if he was being tortured.

Suddenly, I heard muffled footsteps that seemed to be coming closer on the other side of the door. Heart pounding, I quickly hurried back downstairs to my room.

Damn, how could I be so insensitive? Giving him a hard time about not trying therapy when he clearly had been injured. He was still coping with so much physical pain that maybe he couldn't even begin to deal with his emotional pain.

I vowed to just try to live in the here and now, be more sensitive and less anxious, and not interrogate him. No more rules, from him or from me. I would for once allow myself to be in the moment.

GRADY

I'd been up all night fighting the sandman. Maybe it was the altitude or maybe it was all this tension with Isa, but whatever it was, I was fucking miserable. My already short-circuited nerve endings prickled my skin, my head pounded, and my stomach churned.

I snuck downstairs and was shocked to notice that Isa's bedroom door was wide open when the other night it had been shut.

She eventually emerged from her room, her hair wild, her skin flushed. My cock rose to attention.

"Did I oversleep?"

"No, babe. It's fine. What would you like to do today?"

She yawned and sat on the sofa, her nipple buds

pressing against her tank top. "I was thinking we could just get brunch."

Fuck. I'd been hoping for Chinese takeout, Netflix, and sex. I didn't want to leave the safe confines of this cabin and risk having an episode. But I wanted to make her happy. "Sounds good. There's a great restaurant on the water in South Lake Tahoe."

"Okay. Great. I'm going to take a shower and get ready."

I showered in my room, dressed, and waited downstairs for her.

"Woman, we're leaving in five fucking minutes. Get your sexy ass down here."

Isa ran down the stairs, her hair framing her heart-shaped face. Tight jeans showed off her perky ass and it took every ounce of strength not to throw her over the dining room table and take her right then and there. Claim her as mine forever.

I smacked her on the ass and gave her a kiss. It was a sweet, normal moment, like she was my girlfriend.

I locked up the Tahoe home, a gnawing in my stomach. I hadn't been out in public unmasked for months, outside of my doctors' appointments, military check-ins, and that quick run to the store yesterday. She clutched my hand, as if she could sense my discomfort.

We climbed into the truck and made a pit stop to feed our caffeine addictions.

We drove in silence for around forty minutes as Isa took in the scenery and I zoned out to the music.

But something was bothering me. My gut felt she was hiding something, and I really wanted to get to know her better. Time to do some intel. "So tell me about your mom."

Her brow furrowed. "Why do you want to know?"

"I read online that you found her body. Did they ever catch the guy who killed her?"

"What makes you think it was a guy?" Her voice was sharp and irritated.

"Because men are more likely to kill people."

She bit her lip. "What, are you a cop now? Why do you care so much?"

Fuck it. "For someone who thinks I need therapy, you sure get angry when the tables are turned. Forget I asked."

She lowered the window and exhaled. "Sorry. I just don't like to talk about it."

I understood. Completely. "It's fine. So what about your ex-partner? Is he still hung up on you?"

"Pasha? No, we never dated. We danced together as teens, won some championships. He wanted to be a professional dancer, and I didn't. We ended our partnership when I left the show, which is for the best. He wasn't there for me when my mom died and didn't defend me to the tabloids when they were printing lies about me. We're not friends or anything, but we don't hate each other."

I studied her face. She spoke flatly, little emotion toward her memory of him, a guy she'd spent years with pursuing her dreams. It made me think she was cold, closed off. Same way she was with me. Only time she'd been raw with me was when she'd admitted that she'd stolen my bullet. I was used to overly emotional women. "Have you had serious boyfriends?"

Now she turned away from me, gazing distantly. "Not really. I dated some guy my first year of college but it didn't work out. No major drama. What about you? Have you ever had a serious relationship?"

I pounded back my coffee. It was my fault for walking into this line of questioning. I actually hated hearing about a woman's exes, imagining them fucking her. But I'd only asked her because I wanted to see if we had the same views on relationships. Wasn't this what all women wanted? Intimacy? Fine, I'd play. "Once. We started dating before I'd deployed. I thought I was in love at the time, but it was bullshit. She couldn't stand the sight of me after my injuries, not that I could blame her."

Now she turned her attention back to me, her hand placed firmly on my thigh.

"I'm sorry. But Grady, it's in your head. You know that, right?"

"What's in my head?"

"Your perception that no one could love you because of your appearance. I'm sure most people see you how I see you—strong, sexy, masculine, invincible. I just want you to know that no matter what happens with us, I think any woman would be so lucky to have you in her life."

She caressed my face and I resisted the urge to kiss her. I wouldn't allow her to penetrate my soul, get under my skin. Her words were nice to hear, but I refused to believe them; they couldn't possibly be true. I was afraid to let myself care about her, because I was still certain she would eventually leave.

I pushed her hand off of me, accelerated the truck and sped down the freeway. Being around Isa was just like being stuck in one of my PTSD group therapy appointments, but at least it had the added hope of sex. I didn't want to have to think about my feelings, about the past, about my buddies. I only wanted to forget.

We pulled into the parking lot of the Riva Grill. I wished for a second that I had a mask to wear. I adjusted my baseball cap lower on my face, pressed my sunglasses down, and prepared to face the world.

Isa attempted to open her door, but I stopped her. I jumped out of my truck and walked around to open it for her.

She smiled and hopped out of the truck. I wanted to spoil her, make her feel like a princess. Show her that I could be a normal guy.

I took her arm and we walked through the little shops on the way to the restaurant. My eye scanned the tourists, assessing any threats. I couldn't help myself.

A little boy around three years old pointed at me, "Mama, is he monster?"

His mom shushed him, gave me a sympathetic smile, and pulled him toward her. I kept my chin up, not knowing how to respond. Isa's grip remained tight on my arm.

The hostess seated us, a table with a view of the dock. I would've preferred a secluded booth.

As we were perusing our menus, someone dropped a glass behind me. My heart raced. All my nerve endings prickled as adrenaline jolted my system. I clenched my hands into fists around the menu, struggling to keep my breath anywhere close to steady. This was a mistake. I needed to go home.

Isa took my hand. "Are you okay?"

Despite the riot battling inside my body, I replied, "Yup."

We ordered, and as I was sipping my beer and feeling a little calmer, I heard a voice behind me.

"Excuse me, sorry to bother you. Are you by any chance Sergeant Grady Williams?"

I turned around and saw a tall man with white hair wearing a red Marine Corps cap.

"Yes, sir. I am."

"Well, son, it's an honor to meet you. I told my wife it was you when you walked in the restaurant. A real American hero, that's what I said. Would you mind if I took a picture with you?"

I couldn't say no; I had a soft spot for old Marine vets. "Of course not, sir."

His wife snapped a picture of us, the flash momentarily blinding me. The gentleman turned his attention to Isa. "You must be a special young lady to be with a man like Grady."

I sat back down and the waitress brought our food. Isa was glowing.

"Wow, how cool was that? People worship you."

"He's probably a vet. I was happy to take a picture with him, but I really hate the attention."

"Oh, I understand. I used to hate it too, but I guess I eventually became used to it."

I wanted to finish my food and get out of here

before my anxiety heightened and I freaked the fuck out. I sipped my beer, hoping no one else would recognize me.

After we shared a peach cobbler, I was ready to bounce. I called the waitress over and asked for the bill.

"That gentleman took care of your bill. He told me how you saved all these lives in Iraq."

Wow, that had never happened to me before. I turned to thank the gentleman, but he'd gone. I threw down a tip and walked out with Isa.

We looked into a gift shop, which was randomly filled with patriotic toys, so I bought her a Marine Corps bear that sang the Marine Hymn. I checked my watch and realized we needed to get back to the lake house before sunset.

I'd been avoiding sunsets since Iraq, unable to handle the triggers that reminded me of the night my life, as I knew it, ended.

I opened the truck door for her, and she climbed in. Before I closed the door, she wrapped her arms around me. "Thanks, Grady, for bringing me here. It's so beautiful."

She was so beautiful. I was stretching my comfort zone for her, but I couldn't shake the sense that our next public outing wouldn't be so easy.

GRADY

I opened Isa's door the next morning and watched her sleep. Her chest heaved and she made these cute little sighs. I didn't want to sleep next to her, afraid something would startle me and I'd wake up with my hands wrapped around her throat, thinking she was an enemy. I hadn't allowed myself to sleep next to a woman since my injury.

Isa stretched in the bed and opened her eyes. Her lips widened into a smile when she saw me. "Good morning."

"Good morning, sexy."

The doorbell rang, and Isa jumped.

"Are you expecting anyone?" she asked, her voice weak.

"Nope." I stood up and walked over to the security

cameras. Some young, cheese-dick-looking guy stood outside. Despite the fact that it was eighty degrees, this douchebag wore a black V-neck shirt, skinny jeans, and a fitted leather jacket. Once his face came into focus, I recognized him as Pasha, Isa's ex partner.

Isa came over to me and peeped over my shoulder. "That's Pasha, my old partner. What on earth is he doing here?"

I gritted my teeth. "How does he even know you're here? Do you still talk to this guy?"

Isa's eyes widened. "No." Her face turned blush. "But . . . I did see him recently. I went to the studio to ask Benny, the producer, if he could help get me on the show so I could pay for my tuition but he wasn't there. Pasha was though. He said there was no way, unless some celeb requested me." She paused and I was certain she was keeping something from me. "But that was before I asked you about my dad writing your memoir. I haven't spoken to him since that day."

So had she been able to get on the show, I probably would've never seen her again. She asked me about the book because she was desperate and had no choice. Fine, I refused to let that bother me. We were here now, and I was going to try my damnedest to make her happy.

"Don't worry, babe, I'll handle him."

I opened the door. His skin was tight and my first

thought was that he resembled an alien. It immediately struck me that his pale blue eyes seemed hollow. His mouth stretched into a sleazy smile, and he eye-fucked Isa openly. Hell, no. I wanted to deck him, but I controlled my temper.

He stuck out his hand to me. "It is the pleasure to meet together with you, Grady. I'm Pasha Gravilov."

I shook his hand, noting that his grip was weak and insincere.

He embraced Isa in an awkward hug, and she quickly escaped his grasp and clung to my side.

"Privet, *Bellichka*. Now I understand it is that you rejected the offer from me"

What offer? Isa squeezed my arm and whispered to me. "He asked me to teach at his studio." She turned to Pasha, her body remaining by my side. "How on earth did you know I was up here? Did you just drive up from L.A.?"

He let out a deep laugh. "I went to see your old man and he told to me where it is I find you. I am smart man so I put two and two together." He put his hand on my shoulder. "Only reason you did agree to work together with her dad is to get to Bella, *da*?"

I stared Pasha down. "That's it, buddy. I'm not sure why you're here, but it's time for you to leave before I throw you out."

Pasha ignored me, plowed past us, and made himself right at home, sitting on the sofa.

"It is a beautiful place, Grady."

"Why are you here exactly? I'm giving you five minutes before I kick your ass out."

He slicked his hand through his greasy hair. "What is it your plans with the Marines?"

Here we go.

"I'm getting medically retired. After that, no clue."

His gaze shifted. He wanted something from me. "The producer, he has his eye on you. You could do show, dance with beautiful woman, make money. How does that sound?"

I swallowed hard; though I could barely understand him with his thick accent and broken English, I knew one thing for sure—this guy saw me as a meal ticket, just like Isa had seen me as a pity fuck. "I'm not interested. I just want to find something that makes me as happy as being a Marine does. This book is a one-shot deal with me. I'm not going to be your right-wing gun-toting show pony."

I glanced over at Isa, who shook her head and muttered something under her breath.

Pasha let out a cackle that reminded me of the bleats from the goats in Iraq. "Grady, listen to me. You will get money, endorsements, TV shows. I can *make* you."

Fuck, I already told this guy no. For a second, I wondered if Isa put him up to this shit—a way to get her back on the show. But the scowl on her face told me she was as angry with him being here as I was. I needed to get this prick to leave. "Not happening."

"Dammit, just leave him alone," Isa said in a sharp tone.

He leveled her with an icy scowl. "Bella, stay out of this. This is not concerning to you. Why do you not shut up and let the men talk together about business. Go pour me a coffee."

Isa shot a cold, dead glare at him. "Fuck you, Pasha."

Fuck this dude. I didn't give a rat's ass that he was on TV or he used to dance with Isa. No one was going to talk to her like that in front of me.

I grabbed him by the arm and tossed him off the sofa. "Isa's my woman, not yours anymore. Get the fuck out of here."

"Your woman?" Pasha's eyes widened as he straightened his clothes. "You must be blind, also. A woman as beautiful as Bella can never love a man as hideous as you. She's using you for money—just like she used me to dance."

My hands wrapped around his neck and I shoved him against the door. "I may be blind in one eye but you must be deaf. You have no idea who you're dealing with. You contact either of us again and I'll break both your legs and you'll never dance again."

I released him, and he slumped to the floor. This motherfucker wasn't worth going to jail over.

He clenched his fist. "Good job, Bella—you will never get back on show. You left dancing together with me and now want to date this freak?" He slowly stood up. "And Grady, if you lay your hands on me again, I will have you arrested for assault."

Ha. That was almost funny. "Assault? Go right ahead—that will be great for your public image— arrest a war hero who you begged to go on your pathetic show. I'm not afraid of you. Fuck you and fuck your show. What are you going to do? Sue me? I don't have a fucking dime to my name and I'm about to get kicked out of the Corps. I jumped on a grenade to save my buddies' lives—I'll do whatever it takes to protect what's mine, and that includes Isa. If you come by here or harass us, or you talk to her like that again, I'm going to fuck you up. Am I clear?"

His head made a slow, disbelieving shake. "Crystal. I let myself out."

Isa bit her nails, her eyes glued to her feet. I put my arm around her as her ex-partner slammed the door.

I locked the door and set the alarm, then turned

my attention back to Isa. Her hands were clutching her stomach.

"Hey. It's okay." I pressed my hand under her chin.

She gulped. "He's just such a jerk. He only cares about himself. Always has."

I stroked her hair. "Forget about him. I got you."

"No, you don't understand. He has a reason to hate me. He's still mad because I ended our partnership right before Blackpool. We probably would've finaled that year."

"He doesn't matter." I planted a kiss on her forehead. "I'm not going to let anything happen to you."

She sobbed in my arms.

After a few minutes, she abruptly stood up. "I'm going to go take a bath."

I remembered the night I'd met her at the party, how her friend had ditched her. She hadn't mentioned anyone else close in her life. My gut told me, that as of today, I was the only one she had.

ISA

*A*fter seeing Pasha, I wanted to escape, drown out the voices in my head that told me that somehow our partnership had been responsible for my mother's death. I'd been so wrapped up with the show and training for Blackpool that I hadn't noticed how lost my mom was. Maybe I would've seen a sign.

Enough—he didn't deserve to occupy my thoughts. And nothing good came from wondering what if.

I filled the tub with hot water. A large window looked out to the lake, the snowcapped mountains in the distance. I undressed and slipped into the blissful heat.

The best distraction from Pasha was fantasizing about Grady.

Everything was happening so fast between us. It seemed like a big jump to me though, going from never leaving the house, to eating at a restaurant, to spending all our time together. I hoped Grady could handle it, and that he wasn't moving too fast.

Grady opened the door, and I couldn't help but gasp even though I'd seen him only a few minutes ago. Every time I looked at him, he became more and more beautiful to me. His battle scars made him look rougher, tougher, badder.

His eyes focused on my body. I wanted him so badly, I arched my back and made sure to give him a view of my breasts.

His tongue darted out to lick his lips and I imagined his tongue doing its magic on me. "Can I join you?"

"I'd like that." I watched him peel his clothes off, a private strip tease. I'd never grow tired of staring at his body, like some lovesick teenager. His cut abs, his massive chest, his huge biceps. Had he never been injured, his gorgeous face would've matched his incredible body. Who would he be now? Some cocky, drop-dead gorgeous player?

He climbed in the soaker tub and wrapped his body around mine as I relaxed into his. Grady's hands gripped my thighs, and the warmth from his body sparked joy deep inside me.

He squeezed me tight. "I'm glad you dressed as Black Widow that night."

"Me too."

His lips crashed onto mine, and my body became alive next to his. I couldn't get enough of his touch, his scent, his strength.

"Grady, I'm crazy about you."

He let out a growl but kept my body faced away from his, his cock pressing against my ass. "Don't move."

He jumped out of the tub, and the sight of his ass, muscular and defined, was almost enough to send me over the edge. He dimmed the lights, opened a drawer, grabbed a lighter, and lit the candles placed around the tub. He poured some bubble bath in the tub, and turned on the water.

After what seemed way longer than a few minutes, he finally slipped back behind me, and I leaned back into his chest. Our breath syncopated, and his fingers began to massage my temples.

I was practically melting into him when he finally turned the water off. The scent of salted caramel bubble bath filled the room. Grady grabbed a teal mesh loofah and gently kneaded my skin. The fabric danced over my neck, my breasts, down my belly, until it rested in between my thighs. I let out a moan, as his fingers replaced the fabric, teasing my folds, pressing on my clit.

"You're so beautiful, Isa. Let me worship you."

He propped me up on the edge of the tub, knelt in the water, and spread my legs. One hand rubbed my nipples, now slippery and slick, while his other hand teased my pussy.

I was desperate for his tongue, remembering how amazing it felt the other night. His eyes looked up at me, and he flashed a wicked grin before his mouth covered my slit.

His tongue swirled around my lips as he rubbed my clit. The pressure was divine, the perfect blend of sucking and licking.

I released a breath and paused to create a mental picture of this moment and freeze it in time. The peaceful lake, the majestic mountains, the sunlit sky.

My pleasure was pulsing in waves, and I began to moan. Grady seemed invigorated by my response, but instead of continuing, he pulled me off the edge of the tub.

I was sure he was about to fuck me, maybe bent over on the edge of the tub, but he had other plans. One press of the Jacuzzi buttons, and I trembled with anticipation.

"Come here, Isa. I'm gonna make you come so hard."

He positioned me so I was kneeling inside the tub, the jets blasting between my legs.

"Oh, ohmigod."

He slapped my ass, and I moaned. The palm of his hand tweaked my nipples as the rapid stream of water blasted my clit.

"That's it, baby, come for me."

I rolled my hips against the waves, and Grady pushed me flat against the jet.

"Oh my God!" The surge of water unleashed the most intense orgasm I'd ever had. I was out of my mind, riding the pleasure. I screamed Grady's name, and he held me as I collapsed into his arms.

After I came back down to earth, I couldn't stop laughing, delirious with pleasure. I reached to stroke his cock, eager to return the favor, but he just pushed my hand away. "I'm good. I just wanted to make you feel good." He kissed my neck, and we relaxed into the bubbles. "That was the sexiest thing I've ever seen."

I'd never in my life experienced with anyone else the type of chemistry I had with Grady. That instant lust, that mad obsession, that constant longing. I knew what Grady and I had wasn't love, it was something else. Something intoxicating.

And it terrified me.

ISA

*G*rady took off shortly after our sexy time in the bathtub. He said he had a few errands to run and to just make myself at home.

I enjoyed the solitude—I picked a book to read, watched an old *Dateline,* and worked on my needlepoint.

When he returned in the early evening, he finally allowed me to make dinner for him. It was so nice to cook for someone.

After dinner, Grady relaxed in his chair, drinking his beer, his eyes steady on me. "The enchiladas were great. I didn't expect you to be such a good cook."

"Thanks. My mom used to make them for us. They were my dad's favorite." It was one of the last things she had done before she died—taught me all her family recipes. I remembered being so happy bonding with her, never anticipating that she had already made the decision to leave us.

He stood up, told me to wait for a second, and went upstairs. He emerged from his room a few minutes later clutching a shoebox. "I bought you something."

My heart leapt the second I saw telltale suede sole.

"Dance shoes?"

"Yup. I remember watching you dance on the show when I was in the hospital. You were really good." His lips widened, and half of his face seemed to smile.

"It was years ago. I'm sure I've forgotten how to dance." But I quickly realized that was a lie. I remembered everything. Every arch of my foot, every beat of the rhythm, every sway of my back.

"The lady at the store told me these were the best. I looked at your shoes to get the right size."

I wanted to kiss him. I hadn't had new dance heels in years, and my old ones had been danced in until their soles were so barren that I would stub my toes on the floor. Even though I'd had money when I was on the show, those shoes were my lucky shoes. My mom had given them to me. "You shouldn't have. I really don't need them. I don't even dance anymore. That was really sweet of you, but I can't accept them."

He walked over to me and knelt at my feet. His hand reached around my calf, and he took off my flip-flops and rubbed my toes.

I held back a moan. The touch of his hand on my feet made my flesh tingle. The second I slipped my arched foot into the three-and-a-half-inch Latin suede dance shoes, my heart sang, my body yearning to return to the floor.

"Thank you. I love them." We stood up and I wrapped my arms around his neck. His strong arms encircled my waist, and for a moment, I thought he would kiss me. But he released me instead.

Grady went to the formal dining room, and started pushing the table and chairs to the walls.

"Wh-what are you doing?"

He didn't answer.

My mind was still trying to process that this gruff man, the one who barely wanted to talk to me a few days ago, was the same one who would buy me such a thoughtful gift. I was so overwhelmed that it took me a few minutes to realize what he was doing.

He was making me a ballroom.

"Let me see you dance."

"I—I don't have any music."

"Name a song."

I contemplating picking a cool song to impress

him but just decided to go with a classic rumba. "'I'm Not Giving You Up' by Gloria Estefan."

He fiddled on his phone and then plugged it into a speaker.

Grady placed a lone chair in the corner of the room. "Dance for me."

Once the first note of the haunting rumba played, I knew I was back like I'd never skipped a day. That was the universal truth for dancers. No matter what the reason was you quit, no matter how many times you swore you would never return, one step onto that dance floor and your soul became whole again.

My body remembered every rhythmic rumba beat, my toes recalled every jive flick, and my arms reminisced every time I'd placed them in a paso doble battle pose. My gut wrenched—I'd had no clue how much I'd missed this part of my life.

But my reclaimed joy terrified me. One tap of my toes on the sprung hardwood floor, and I wanted to lose myself in the music.

My toes traced the floor during the rumba walks, my core settled into the beat. I danced as much for Grady as I did for myself.

Grady focused on me, his gaze steady, never looking away. Over the years I'd danced for so many people, in many shows and competitions, but I never had danced solely for the eyes of one man.

My man.

I danced toward him, shimmied my hips near his face, teasing him gently. I wasn't a stripper, this wasn't a lap dance, but the energy between us was passionate. I yearned for him to stand up, take me on the floor, expose his secrets to me.

I turned away from him, but his strong arms pulled me back. He pushed me onto his lap, grinding me down on his hard cock. His hand pulled my hair, pressing me into his lips. I kissed him back, high off the urgency, his beard tickling my skin. His lips were powerful yet soft, just like him. All my misgivings about getting close to him were fading, as I was melting into him. Our kiss was equal parts illicit and comforting. But the intensity of my emotions spooked me—I pushed him off of me, tears welling in my eyes.

As the song ended, emptiness filled me. My body chilled. One taste of my obsession with the beat, and I'd be drowning in a sea of rhinestones before I could help myself. Like an addict in recovery, I feared I'd be unable to quit after one dance.

And I knew I'd be unable to quit Grady after our time together was over.

GRADY

I loved watching Isa dance, the way her body swayed with the music, as if she was dancing just for me.

But I needed a change of scenery.

As much as I loved the lake house, the place was a bit too pretentious for me. I wanted to be out in the wilderness, camping in nature. Luckily Isa was game, so the next day after lunch, we drove to a local campground that had small cabins. It was beautiful, so rustic, so removed from the world. This place was simple, humble, and more my style. It reminded me of vacationing in the Smoky Mountains in Tennessee. The cabin we rented here was unfortunately named "The Honeymoon Cabin." It was constructed with knotty pine, contained a simple stove, a refrigerator, a small table, a sofa, and a queen bed made up with a pinecone quilt. Outside on the pine needle-covered ground were a barbecue, picnic table, and campfire pit.

We checked in and relaxed in the cabin for a bit. I'd planned to grill some burgers, down a few beers, and then spend all night fucking Isa.

But she had other plans.

"Wow, it's gorgeous up here, Grady. Let's go on a walk around the campsite."

I hesitated. It was seventeen hundred. A gorgeous, late summer sunset.

I suddenly had a strong urge to remain in the cabin. But I chose not to listen to my gut. I could do this.

"Sure."

I wrapped my arms around her slender waist and went outside. For the first few minutes, I enjoyed the mountain air, the sweet, smoky smell of ribs from a neighboring barbecue, the comfortable silence between Isa and me. We walked around the grounds, weaving in between cabins, trees, picnic tables, and a tiny creek.

Then it happened again.

The roar of plane engines overhead, the towering mountains in the distance, the scent of dust mixed with diesel, the chill of the wind on my face, the haunting glow of the sunset highlighting the sky.

I choked on the air and fear penetrated my soul.

Fuck.

The perfect blend of the elements had triggered every sense in my core.

The rapid beating of my heart pulsed through my chest.

My gut clenched and dread overtook me. Like some fucked up time warp, my mind was back in Iraq, trapped in an eternal hell that I could never escape.

"Grady, you okay?"

But I could barely hear her words—my ears were echoing with my screams, the screams of my fellow Marines. I could see Rafael's face as the bullet hit him, his brains splattered around me. The heat of the bomb underneath me. Counting down until my death.

10. 9. 8. 7. 6. 5. 4. 3. 2. 1.

I needed to get the fuck out of here. But no matter where I went, I would never flee this terror.

But almost as soon as it had started, my flashback was over.

Fuck.

"Grady, babe, let's go back."

I wiped the sweat beads from my forehead with my clammy hands and attempted to steady my breathing. My fingers tore at my clothes, ripping my shirt, wanting to relieve the pressure from my chest.

Flashback. I'd had another flashback. They'd never go away. This was my new reality; my fucked up brain didn't respond to any of the drugs or talk therapy I'd been given. In the movies or in books, it was made to seem like flashbacks were movies in one's mind or images of dead friends. Yes, I relived that night vividly in my nonstop nightmares. Though I couldn't speak for all other vets, for me a flashback was more than a film playing in my head. Sights, scents, sounds. A primal feeling that I was in grave danger, that I would never be safe, that everyone I loved would be taken from me. That I was helpless. As if I were entombed in an unbreakable dark box underwater, suffocating and gasping for air. All taking me back to a night I didn't want to remember, to a night I'd never forget.

ISA

I grasped Grady's hand, and the sweat from his palms seeped into mine. His face registered a blank stare and I could see his breath in the cold evening air puffing short, labored breaths.

Within minutes, we were back at the cabin. Grady sat in a chair and I turned the stove on to make him tea.

He exhaled. "I'm sorry, I—" His words were sharp and staccato.

I cut him off. "No, babe, you have nothing to be sorry about. We don't have to talk about it unless you want to."

I wanted to talk. I wished I could climb into his mind and erase his memories of war.

Maybe he could return the favor. Erase the memories of seeing my mom dead. Erase the memories of what I knew.

We could both start fresh, no pasts, both of us could learn to be present and just be here now.

But that was impossible. All I could do was comfort him. Try to put down my walls too. Allow myself to fall in love with him and be loved back.

His hands finally stopped shaking.

"Are you okay?"

"Sure."

Sure. Didn't sound convincing but I'd take it. The teakettle whistled and I poured two cups of hot water. I dunked the tea bags into the mugs, watching the warm liquid turn to a dark amber shade, then placed the cup in front of Grady.

We sat in silence, sipping our tea. He had access to the best care, but clearly, however they were treating him, wasn't working.

He finally spoke, his words disjointed. "Sunset. Late summer sunset, a night like this. Mountains, a chill in the air, planes overhead."

Triggers. I couldn't even pretend to imagine what it was like to be in a combat zone. Or to feel like you'd never left.

I'd studied every published detail of his attack available after I met Grady—hell I could recite his medal citation from memory.

Without hesitation and with complete disregard for his own safety, Corporal Williams reached out and pulled the grenade to his body, shielding his fellow Marines only feet away. When the grenade detonated, his body absorbed the brunt of the blast, severely wounding him, but saving the life of his fellow Marines. By his undaunted courage, bold fighting spirit, and unwavering devotion to duty in the face of almost certain death, Corporal Williams reflected great credit upon himself and upheld the highest traditions of the Marine Corps and the United States Naval Service.

I wanted to hear about what he went through in his own words. Maybe it would even help him, to talk about the night, desensitize it. I certainly wasn't a trained psychologist. But Grady and I had something —whatever we labeled it—between us. Maybe he could share with me what he couldn't tell others.

"Grady, that's fine if you don't want to talk about it, I understand. But if you'd like to tell me, I'd really like to know what happened to you."

He sighed and stared in the distance. "We were clearing houses, looking for terrorists. This one motherfucking insurgent threw a grenade in front of my Marines. I jumped on the grenade."

He said it matter-of-factly, like it wasn't a big deal, like he bought the guy behind him a drink at Starbucks. "Why?"

His voice lowered. "Because it was my job.

Because I'm a Marine. Because he was my best friend, my brother in arms, I loved him. He would've done it for me. I was just the unlucky motherfucker to be in the wrong place at the wrong time. And the worst thing about it . . . he died anyway. I did it all for nothing."

I wanted more, so much more. To go deep into his psyche. Find out every detail about the night, what he saw, what he felt, physically and emotionally. But not like this, not yet.

I turned into him and initiated a kiss. He kissed me back, but these kisses weren't lustful. They were comforting, dare I say soothing, or possibly even loving.

I pulled back for a moment, and looked at him, really saw him. I imagined what he had looked like before the injury, who he had been before he'd sacrificed his looks, his health, his soul. Was it for his country? Was it for his friend?

Tears welled in my eyes.

His gaze was fixated on me too, and I allowed him to look at me. To truly see me. Did he see my longing for him? How much I wanted to be loved by him? How hard I prayed that this, whatever *this* was, could possibly work out?

He lifted me off the chair and carried me to the bed. It creaked when he placed me on the quilt, and we both laughed. It was nice to see him smile, a hint of joy brightening his face.

He climbed on top of me as his lips took mine again. His tongue slowly explored my mouth as his hand guided down my body.

I wiggled out of my clothes as he pulled off his shirt. His arm reached around to unhook my bra, and his mouth lapped at my breasts, the stubble from his beard rubbing against my chest.

I decided to take a risk—put myself out there and let him know what I was feeling. I whispered in his ear, "I'm falling in love with you." Tonight, there was a sense of comfort between us, as if every kiss was healing our souls.

He pulled down my panties, and I heard the distinct sound of foil ripping. His tip grazed me and pressed between my legs. This teasing was unbearable; I couldn't wait any longer. I'd never wanted anyone more in my life.

His lips locked again with mine as he pushed deep inside me. His pace alternated between hunger and caution, as if he was holding back the beast within. I wasn't scared of his wild side; I wanted to see the animal he kept caged. I pulled him closer to me, urging him to fill me up and erase the space between us.

He glided in and out of me, each thrust taking me

closer to nirvana. He paused for a second and looked deep in my eyes.

"I need you."

Need? That was good, right? It had to mean something. I needed him too; I needed this moment, this feeling.

His fingers interlaced with mine and he pinned them over my head. His pace quickened, and I could feel myself desperately trying to hold on to the cliff, hold on and ride the waves of ecstasy. He released my hands, and I clutched the sheets as he ground deep inside me, pressing flat against my belly, giving me the direct stimulation I craved. I dug my fingers into his ass, and he pounded into me. Our release came crashing down around us, and I savored every second as our bodies drowned together in a sea of satisfaction.

This man loved his fellow Marines, was willing to give his life for them. He was capable of loving someone more than he loved himself. I wondered what it would be like to be loved by such a man.

But my heart was restless. Soon our world would change, our time out here would be over. No matter how much we wanted to, we would never be able to return to the innocence of this moment.

GRADY

I stood up, grabbed my pillow, and placed it on the sofa, ready to sleep alone when she grabbed my arm.

Her eyes pleaded with me. "Can I spend the night with you? I really want to try to make this work."

Of course I wanted her to sleep with me, to fuck her sweet pussy every night, though I wasn't sure if that emotional performance she just gave was nothing more than a combination of an apology for her ex-partner insulting me and pity after witnessing my flashback. At this point I didn't care what her motivations were—I just wanted her near me.

"Sure. Just promise me you'll wake me if I scream in my sleep." I tossed my pillow back on the bed and climbed under the covers with her. "I'm glad you begged me to let your dad write my book. I honestly would've never done it. And I'm actually looking forward to saving up some money. The VA sucks and who knows if I'll be able to hold down a job. And I'll get to tell my side of the story in the book."

She rolled on top of me, staring into my eye. "The book will be amazing. Get some!"

I kissed her forehead, appreciative of her Marine Corps "get some" reference, as if she was trying to relate to me.

In my post-coital haze, I decided to put myself out there even more. It had gone well so far. No more games. From here on out, I wanted her to know she's mine.

"For the ball, I don't want you to pretend to be my girlfriend."

"Oh?"

I lifted up her hand and kissed it. "I want you to *be* my girlfriend." Once the words left my mouth, I knew I had made the right decision asking her. Since I'd left the hospital, I'd stopped making plans for the future. I wanted to look forward to my life—with Isa in it.

A big smile spread across her face, and her eyes sparkled.

"Yes." She wrapped her arms around my neck, a shot of adrenaline reinvigorating me.

She pursed her lips like she was thinking. "Grady, since this is a ball, do you know how to dance?"

"Nope. Never learned."

"Well, can I teach you? Just two dances. Maybe a foxtrot and a rumba? I really had a great time dancing last night."

Hell no. "Nope, not going to happen. Most Marines just end up screwing around, you might see them dancing to 'YMCA' or the electric slide, but no one really dances."

"I get that. But I mean the President will be there. You're the guest of honor. And once the press finds out you're going with me, they're going to expect something. Especially since we're dating."

I tensed up my shoulders. Writing a book was one thing—I wasn't going to learn how to dance. "No. It would be like a gateway drug. Next thing you know I'd be on *Dancing under the Stars*."

"Ha!" she laughed. "It's fine. Just thought it would be fun."

She cuddled onto my chest, and I wrapped my arms around her. She fit perfectly. For the first time since I'd met her, I felt like there was a possibility that she could truly need me.

"Fine, two dances, that's it. I'm not wearing those weird shoes with heels. And don't get any crazy ideas about waxing my chest and stuffing me in a rhine-stone onesie."

She giggled. "You're hilarious Grady. Okay—it's a deal."

Damn, this woman had me whipped already.

GRADY

The next morning we left the campsite and headed back to the cabin. We had a few more days here before we would return to the real world.

In the daylight, I was filled with embarrassment that she'd seen me have another flashback. She'd been understanding and comforting, but I was worried that the novelty would wear off and she wouldn't be able to deal with my issues long term.

We arrived back home and we milled around the cabin in silence. I needed to know why she'd snapped at me earlier in the week when I asked about her mother's death.

I went to the kitchen and poured her a mug of

coffee. After a few minutes, she sat at the table with me.

"So what happened to your mom?"

She looked away from me, her face turning red. "She died. End of story."

I didn't have a clue how to read women. Men were direct. If a dude had a problem with someone, he'd kick his ass, share a beer later when it was resolved. I hated playing the guessing game with this girl. "Cut the bullshit. You say you want to get to know me, but you're being secretive. I absolutely can't stand liars. You lied to me about where I'd seen you before, and you snapped at me when I asked about your mom. Just please be honest with me."

Her hand was shaking. "It doesn't matter how she died—it only matters that she is dead."

I would get this girl to open up to me. I put my arm around her, her petite body fitting perfectly on my chest. "Babe, you have to trust me."

She just looked away from me. For the first time it occurred to me that she might be in as much pain as I was. I had nothing left to lose—I'd lost my best friend, my career, I'd almost lost my life—twice. Once from a grenade, and another time from my own hands. I would lay my heart open for her sake.

I raised her chin with my thumb. "Fine, I'll go first. I need to thank you for taking that bullet out of my gun. A few days after we met, I found out I was getting kicked out of the Corps. It was really dark for me. I'm in so much fucking pain all the time, I miss my buddy who died in the attack. I felt worthless. So I tried to end it. You're the reason I'm standing here today. So, thank you."

She gripped the sides of her head, as if she was covering her ears. "Oh my God, Grady. I'm so sorry you were suffering, and I'm so grateful I took that bullet. Suicide is never the answer. You're such an amazing man. Your life is so valuable."

I didn't want to hear her fake platitudes. She didn't know anything about the true darkness that lurked within me. "I'm fine now. Don't worry about me. Now it's your turn."

She pulled her knees to her chest, her voice choked with tears. "My mom. She wasn't murdered. She killed herself. I was the one who found her, her brains splattered everywhere."

Bile rose in my throat. So that was what she was hiding from me. And my dumbass had just told her I'd attempted suicide. She'd never want to continue this relationship with me. I was just like her mom. "Man, I'm sorry."

"I couldn't deal with life, the press asking questions about my mom, so I quit the show, hoping the truth wouldn't get out. The tabloids printed crazy rumors that I had some drug problem and that I went to rehab. To this day, I don't know where that rumor started. So that's why I took your bullet. You . . ." Her eyes were teary. "You remind me of her."

Fuck.

I looked in her green eyes, really looked at her, and allowed her to look at me. I didn't turn my head when she stared at my face. If a woman this beautiful could stand the sight of me, if she stood by my side, maybe I could face the world again.

Maybe not.

"I'd be lying if I said I wasn't in pain. The skin grafts are brutal. And my brain is fucked up. I have triggers, and I can't control myself. If I see something that reminds me of that night, I lose it. You've seen me."

"It's hard, I know. Just take your time." She put her hand on my thigh and pursed her lips. "I wish I'd never run out the night we met. I was scared. And the truth is, I couldn't stop thinking about you. About that night."

Her soft touch immediately invigorated me. "Me either, baby."

I reached around her waist and pulled her closer to me. A lock of hair fell in her face and I brushed it back. She looked up at me through her long, black eyelashes, and I couldn't resist a second longer. My lips covered hers, and her warm, sweet tongue danced in my mouth.

Last time I fucked her with the faint hope that it might lead to something more. Tonight, I would fuck her, praying that it would last forever. I could keep her safe, I could love her.

Her delicate hands rubbed the back of my neck as we kissed. We didn't rush our lips. I had some time alone with this girl—I could take all the time I wanted.

Her fingernails scraped my scarred skin, and the sensation sent chills through my body. She lightly kissed my neck, then she nibbled on the nub where my ear used to be. I resisted the urge to shove her mouth away, not wanting her to be disgusted by me. But her lips found a way back to my tortured flesh, and the comfort of her kisses was more soothing than any creams that I had ever applied to my wounds.

My hands gripped her tiny waist. I loved her curvy hips, her round ass. She was perfection. I wanted to pleasure her, worship her, show her that I could be the man to protect her from anyone. If only she'd let me.

She lifted off my shirt, her eyes widening at the sight of my chest. I undressed her beautiful body, slowly, savoring the unveiling of her flesh. The previous times we'd had sex had been laced with lust. Tonight, I wanted to make love to her.

I had nothing left to say. Scooping her in my arms, I carried her into the bedroom. Her eyes widened, and she bit her bottom lip. I'd fantasized about this very moment for the past few weeks, and I was in no rush.

I placed her on my bed and we knelt facing each other. My hand pushed her hair back, and I planted a kiss on her neck. Her skin was so soft and tan. Her lips parted and my mouth took hers, indulging in every sensation of her hot tongue probing my mouth. These kisses were so much better than yesterday's kisses, which were shortly after my PTSD attack, when I was so afraid of losing her.

I was afraid of nothing now.

I cradled her head and urged her closer to me, pressing her clothed body against mine. She kissed my face tenderly as she began to undress me. I removed her white tank top and kissed her cleavage. Her head dropped back and she gave out a sweet sigh. My hand unhooked her bra and then teased her nipples with my fingers, pinching and tugging until her face was flush with pleasure.

"Grady, you're torturing me."

I grinned. Taking her buds, I sucked on one while

my hand squeezed the other. She moaned causing a jolt of pressure to my already hard cock.

Her hands dug into my shoulders and she began kissing my chest, licking my nipples, straddling my waist. I was so desperate to be inside her.

She undid my belt and removed my shorts as I pulled down her sweatpants. She was wearing a mesh lace thong. I teased her with my tongue, tasting her sweet wetness. When I couldn't resist anymore, I pushed her panties down and devoured her pussy.

She writhed on the bed, gasping, moaning, every sound making me want her more. I could eat her pussy for days, forever.

I grabbed a condom from my nightstand, pulled off my boxers, turned her over, and climbed on top of her. Her round ass mesmerized me. I took off her thong and wrapped my arm around her.

"Ready for me?" I whispered into her ear.

"Yes, baby."

I grabbed my cock in my hand and slid into her warm pussy.

The softness of her ass as I pressed deeper heightened my desire. She moved in sync with my thrusts. I rubbed her clit until she was moaning, almost gasping for air. I could feel her pussy clench tight around my cock and I was desperate to release. I pumped faster, harder, deeper, out of my mind in pleasure. She let out a long cry and I came with her.

We collapsed onto the bed, my mind completely blank. I was about to get up when she turned toward me and cupped my face.

We lay in silence and I listened to the pattering of rain falling on the roof.

"Grady, I need to tell you something."

Great, here it goes. I already knew what she was going to say, "I care for you but this isn't going to work"—the usual line of bullshit. I was ready. Bracing myself, I asked, "What?"

"I love you."

ISA

I told Grady I loved him. And he hadn't said it back.

But I wasn't freaking out yet. He'd asked me to be his girlfriend—he'd opened up to me about his depression.

Though honestly, knowing that he had been suicidal filled my heart with more fear than love.

Grady gave me a wicked smile the next day and told me he had the perfect plan for us. I reluctantly agreed—even though I hated surprises.

Grady and I sat in his truck in silence as we drove on the freeway. This entire setup felt so surreal. I wanted a crystal ball so I could read our future. I wanted assurance that we could make some type of relationship work. I had never navigated an adult relationship and I didn't have a clue what I was doing. The tension hung thick in the air, and even the view of the beautiful mountains did little to ease my nerves.

We pulled off a dirt road, and I saw a sign: "Shooting & Safety."

"You're taking me to a gun range?"

"Yup. Since you're an expert and all at disarming weapons."

I shuddered. "You're kidding me. I hate guns. I told you my mom shot herself. Not to mention you confessed to me that you tried to shoot yourself. Nope, not going to happen."

He placed his hand on my thigh and looked at me. "You don't have to shoot, and if you want to, we'll leave. But you're the one always talking about therapy. One of the methods I was taught was to desensitize yourself from the experience. This is a safe place. I want you to take back the power."

"And this from the guy who claims that therapy doesn't work."

"I was blown up by a grenade. I can't really do that again to desensitize myself. But I'm working on other ways to deal with it. Talking to you helps. So does fucking you."

"Funny." I exhaled, happy he could admit that keeping his feelings bottled up was futile.

As we pulled up to the shooting range, my fingers tingled and it wasn't from the cold. I'd been raised shooting with my dad, but after my mom killed herself with his gun, I'd never had a desire to be anywhere near a weapon, though I had made an exception when I stole Grady's bullet.

"Wait here." Grady walked around the truck and opened my door. Swoon. He hoisted me out of the truck.

Once inside the building, he introduced himself to the range owner.

The older gentleman shook his hand. "Sergeant Williams, I assure you that you do not need an introduction. It's an honor to meet you. Thank you for your service."

Grady posed for a few pictures, and I realized that in this environment he was a celebrity. This man was in awe of Grady.

The man placed his arm around me, in a fatherly hug. "Well, ma'am, you're a lucky young lady to have a man like Grady Williams by your side."

The fear pulsed through my veins as the owner pulled me aside to ask if I'd ever shot before.

"Yes, sir, I have but it was years ago. I'll be honest, I'm pretty scared."

"Well, you couldn't have a better teacher. Grady's a legend."

We were led into the shooting area that kind of resembled a really secure bowling alley, long lanes separated by partitions. Grady fitted me with goggles and ear protectors, then his face turned serious. "Okay, Isa. We have some safety rules. First rule, treat every weapon as if it were loaded. Second, never point a weapon at anything you do not intend to shoot. Third, keep your weapon on safety until you're ready to fire. I will walk you through each step. Now, carefully pick up the pistol."

I hesitated to grab the gun, my heart beating rapidly. Grady had brought his own pistol, a matte camouflaged-colored piece of death, which he informed me was a Colt M45.

What had my mom felt before she retrieved my father's gun from the safe? Why had he given her the code? Did she think of me before she blew her brains out?

I choked back tears.

Grady leaned into me. "You okay, baby? You don't have to do this."

I swallowed hard. "No, I'm fine. I want to."

Picking up the gun with my right hand, the cold metal imprinted on my palm. It felt heavy, its deadly steel haunting in my hands. I shivered; I didn't know if I could go through with this. I made sure to keep pointing the gun down range as I drew in a shaky breath.

"Good, baby. Now load the magazine."

With my left hand, I loaded the magazine, careful to not pinch my fingers.

"Great job. Your stance is good, keep your legs parallel, arm extended. You will feel recoil when you shoot. Let it happen. Don't tense up, and keep your weapon pointed in a safe direction."

He wrapped his arms around me, his hands steady, his hard body pressed into mine. He took the weapon and adjusted my hands around it, his hands around my own, as if he was protecting me from the gun.

"You got this, babe. Now just aim and fire. I'm not going to let anything happen to you."

The target was one of those paper bodies with a red heart. My hand slowly pulled back the trigger, and I fired and let out a yelp. The recoil surprised me, but Grady held me firmly in his grasp. A huge wave of relief swept over me.

"Good job, baby. Keep going."

I pressed the trigger again, this time more confident. *Bam, bam, bam, bam.* Electricity pulsed through my veins; my heart beat fiercely. I felt alive, in control, strong, and powerful.

As I rode this new high, I placed the weapon

down, relieved to relinquish its weight, both physical and emotional.

Grady picked up the gun. "Let me show you how it's done."

I took a step back, and Grady fired the weapon over and over. With precision.

Bam, bam, bam.

Every shot dead center. His face was calm, centered, focused. No hesitation.

My mouth dropped. I was so turned on despite myself. How hot was this guy? I'd never had a military fetish, never been attracted to a man who shot guns. But being around this man, this superhero, for once in my life, I felt completely safe.

After he fired the final shot dead center in the imaginary enemy's forehead, he unloaded the magazine, placed his gun in a case, and we walked out of the range.

As we exited the building, he wrapped his arm around my shoulders and kissed me sweetly. Kisses have different purposes in life—some are for lust, some are for pity, some are for love. This one was for comfort. It was tender, dare I say loving. It was an amazing kiss. I had so much to say to him, desperately wanting to tell him more about my mother, but once again I was at a loss for words. Grady always rendered me speechless.

GRADY

*B*eing back on the range today rattled me. I loved shooting—I'd been a rifle coach, had dreamed of being a sniper. The power, the rush, the thrill. It was completely addicting.

But these days, the sound of gunfire brought me back to Iraq. When I'd been over there, it wasn't about the politics, it wasn't about the war. It was about protecting my brothers. One goal; getting them out of there alive.

As I held the gun, I focused on why I loved shooting: the precision, the power, the skill. I refused to allow myself to think of the men I'd killed in combat, refused to picture their faces, and the way their bodies slumped when they hit the ground.

There were some things I'd done that I would never tell Isa.

It was bad enough that I looked like a monster. She would never love me if she knew I was also a killer.

When we returned to the cabin, we relaxed for a bit. After an hour Isa came over to the sofa and sat on my lap. "I'm going to just teach you some fundamentals of dancing. Nothing too intense today."

I grimaced, but I refused to go back on my word. My dance knowledge consisted of doing joke moves to make my Marines laugh—lawn mower, the fishing pole, the hammer. But once I committed to something, I put in one hundred and ten percent. "Sounds good."

"Okay, I'm going to run upstairs and change. Luckily, you bought me dancing shoes."

Yeah, what a stroke of luck. I'd just wanted to see her dance, not to have to dance myself.

I made a fresh pot of coffee and waited for her.

Five minutes later, she walked down the stairs and I almost dropped the coffee pot. She wore a loose purple shirt and multicolored yoga pants that seemed painted on her curvy ass. Instead of tennis shoes, her feet were strapped in the sexy little dance heels.

We cleared the living room so we could use it as a dance floor, and she turned on Sam Smith from her iPhone. The song was soothing and melodic, definitely not like my usual listening choice of heavy metal.

"So, we're going to start with the basics—rumba walks. They're also used in cha-cha and bolero. Keep your toes on the floor, chest up, straight back, and push off of your standing leg."

Her hand adjusted my hip and all I could think about was having her hand drop lower to my cock.

"Good. Okay, that's a good start. Keep your legs straight, when you bring your right leg to your left, settle your hip, and then stick your right leg forward and transfer your weight."

Fuck, this was hard, though she made it look easy. Her hips seemed to be flowing back and forth, as if they were making love to the floor. I was used to drill —precise steps with my feet, syncopated with my fellow Marines.

She taught me a basic rumba, a dance of unrequited love, and a bit of the foxtrot, a dance of happily-ever-afters. Who knew these dances actually had stories behind them?

Isa drilled me relentlessly with the steps and rules —feet on the floor, shoulders down, chest and chin up. After an hour of me following her around the floor like a lovesick puppy, I'd had enough, but I wasn't about to quit. I didn't want to look like an idiot in front of my fellow Marines who would no doubt be egging me on.

"So, I think you have the moves down. But you're still missing something."

"What?"

"We're going to work on our connection in the dance. Our dancing depends on our ability to get our audience to feel our spark."

I thought I had it down, but she was right. There was still something I was missing.

Emotion.

Intimacy.

I had to feel something, something toward Isa, something toward the dance. She'd told me she loved me. Did I love her? I craved her, I was addicted to her, I wanted her to be mine. But I was comfortably numb. I didn't have a clue how to really bond with anyone. After all the losses I'd suffered, it felt too dangerous, too risky, to open myself up to feeling, to caring about someone. What if I lost her too?

She moved her body into my space. "We're going to start with a game. In dance, the man is always in control."

I liked this more and more. "Keep talking."

"I need you to lead me, take charge, own me."

I ran my fingers through my hair. "Fuck, baby, if I

knew dancing was this hot, I would've started years ago."

She gave me a playful glance, untied her hair, which had been wrapped up in one of those weird scarfs, and handed the silky fabric to me. "Here, blindfold me."

What the fuck? "Don't have to ask me twice, sweetheart. I didn't know you were into that sort of thing, but I'd be happy to tie you up and lick your pussy until you can't stop coming."

Her mouth widened into a cautious smile and a nervous laugh escaped her lips. "I'll take a rain check, Hulk. But for now, I need you to blindfold me and lead me around the room. When we're dancing, we can't speak. We can only communicate through movement. And we need to build trust. Though I may be your teacher, on the floor you are always in charge. Make me submit to you."

Heat rose through my body. I couldn't tell if she was fucking with me, but if she was, I didn't care. I didn't hesitate but pulled her to me and secured the scarf around her eyes. Without saying a word, she swiveled her hips into mine and laid her head on my chest.

"Dance with me. Don't think, just connect," she whispered, breathy, sexy.

I wrapped my arms around this beautiful woman

and just moved to the music. When I stepped, she followed, mirroring my every movement, even though she couldn't see. Her fingers brushed my neck, her chest heaved with mine, our legs moved in sync. Our bodies became one unit. I'd always seen dancing as pointless, but I'd never been this physically close to a woman without having sex. It was hot as hell.

After the song finished, I removed her blindfold.

Then she looked up and smiled at me. A genuine smile, accepting, loving. She didn't wince in horror at my face; instead she looked at me the way I'd once prayed that someone, someday, would look at me. Like she loved me.

And I knew one truth in that moment.

"Isa." I cupped her face and looked into her beautiful green eyes. "I love you."

She wrapped her arms around my neck and kissed my face. "I love you, too. You make me so happy."

GRADY

*A*fter an epic night, we decided to take it easy the next morning. We both sat close together on the sofa, catching up on our phones.

Then I saw it.

A text from Trace containing a web link.

Trace: Bro, did u c this?

I clicked on the link which led to a gossip article.

"Bella Applebaum's Deal with the Devil Dog: Why the desperate former reality star agreed to pretend to be the girlfriend of maimed Medal of Honor recipient Grady Williams."

What the fuck?

Rage swept through me as I skimmed the article.

"According to a source, Bella told her friend that she was repulsed by Grady but agreed to attend the Marine Corps Ball with him as long as her father could write Grady's war memoir."

I'd never been under any delusion that my face was anything but grotesque. But reading this article, knowing that she told her someone I disgusted her singed my already scorched skin with humiliation.

I could show her the article, listen to her false apologies, her protests that she never said it, but there was no point. Rejection stung my soul. I'd been wrong about her, wrong about sharing my feelings. I hated myself for being stupid enough to believe she could love me. I wanted her gone—out of my life.

Forever.

In all honesty, I should've never allowed myself to get close to her—from the second I'd first seen her, I'd known she was out of my league. She was too beautiful, too sexy. How could she ever love a beast?

I stood up from the sofa and looked toward the ground. I refused to give her the satisfaction of staring at me again.

"I've made a mistake. This, whatever this was, isn't going to work out. I'll pay for you to change your ticket so you can go home early."

"What? Are you serious? After telling me last night that you love me you want me to go?"

"Yup," I said flatly.

My back was turned to her, but I could hear her stand up. She placed her hand on my shoulder. I pushed it off.

"Don't make this harder than it is. It would never work out between us. And I've decided that I don't want to write a book. Meeting Pasha made me realize that once I start up with celebrity shit, I'll become a fucking puppet."

"No." She wasn't giving up. "I don't care about the book, I'll find another way to pay for my tuition, even if I have to take a year off. I can get a loan. I can get a few jobs. Don't do this, Grady. I'm in love with you! Just because you're scared—"

"Scared? Scared of what? You? Love? You don't know what the fuck you're talking about. You don't know the meaning of the word scared. Get the fuck out of my face. If you want to talk about our relationship, I'm sure your friend would love to hear more stories about how repulsive I am."

Her mouth flew open. "What are you talking about? I never said that."

"Whatever, Isa. Just get your shit and go."

She stormed off to her room, cursing under her breath. I threw my cell phone at the wall, hoping it would shatter. That way, I'd be unreachable. Any minute now my phone would be blowing up with sympathetic texts about that article.

She emerged a few minutes later, clutching her suitcase. "Grady, I read the article. I didn't say that I swear. I told Mirasol that—"

"Doesn't matter. I don't want to hear your excuses. Just stop."

"No, you're going to listen to me. I didn't say that. I said your scars are horrific and clearly you've suffered so much, but you're sexy anyway. Please believe me." Her voice was choked with emotion.

"It's more than that. This will never work. I just want to be alone." And I meant that with every cell in my body. I didn't need this internal anguish, this humiliation. I didn't need her.

I grabbed her luggage. As we walked toward the door, I could sense her mood changing. A scowl graced her face.

But she wasn't my problem.

We walked outside and I loaded her luggage in the car.

She clutched my arm. "Grady, I didn't say that. If you aren't aware already of how the media skews everything, you need a crash course ASAP. You're in the public eye, whether you want to be or not."

"That story is on national news. You still told

someone about our agreement for the book deal, something you told me to keep quiet."

"Yeah, I did. I told my best friend. That's what friends do—they share. And I texted Marisol—she swore to me she didn't say that to the press, and I believe her. I trust her. Someone overheard us and then sold a false story to the tabloids. This happens every day. I can give a statement and it will go away."

I wanted to believe her. But it was too late now. The entire world now saw me as a joke.

She caressed my waist and I wanted to feel her hands on me this one last night.

"You're an amazing guy. You're heroic, strong, sexy, and surprisingly sweet. But you have PTSD. You need help. I can't walk out of here today and regret not telling you how I feel. I think we could really have something beautiful here. We could even have an amazing life together. I love you, but I can't be with you if you don't love yourself. And you don't even want to try. You risk your life to save your friends, but you won't even attempt to save yourself. You're worth it, I'm worth it. If you go get some help, I'll be here when you're finished. If not, I'm not going to the ball with you. Promise or no promise."

I clenched my fist, using every bit of self-control I had to not plunge it into the car door.

"So it's all my fault this won't work? I'm not the only one fucked up here, Isa. You're a mess too. Always trying to save everyone—me, your dad. What makes you happy? What are you running from? Your mom killed herself and you found her—well, that's pretty fucked up. Have you dealt with that? What are you doing to take care of yourself? At least I admit freely that I'm a wreck. That I'll never be able to do the one thing I've wanted to do my entire life—be a sniper. You want to be a clinical psychologist to help people, I get that. But I've seen you dance. Not just here with me, but I used to watch you every week on television with my grandma. And once I discovered who you are, I watched old clips. You loved dancing, you glowed. I've never seen that glow on your face, that light in your life. You claim you want to live your life free and not hide from anyone, but you are hiding from yourself."

Her face reddened and her nostrils flared. I expected a smartass retort, but her silence infuriated me more. She had to know I was right. Instead of trying to help everyone around her, Isa needed to help herself.

Her face softened. "You're right. I'm damaged too, and I miss dancing. But I'm going to do something about it. I hope you will too. And no matter what happens with our relationship, I hope we can remain friends."

Friends? Fuck that, I could never be a friend to a woman I'd fucked. The thought of another man touching Isa, fucking her, killed me.

I gritted my teeth. "Not going to happen. I never want to see you again."

A grimace lingered on her face and her chin trembled. "You don't mean that."

She kissed my scarred cheek, and I resisted the urge to grab her, kidnap her, throw her over my back like a caveman staking his property. Before I knew what had happened, her car disappeared behind the pines.

ISA

I drove away from the lake house, rage, hurt, love, and guilt consuming me. I bit my nails, sped on the freeway, and blasted music.

How dare Grady try to psychoanalyze me? Maybe he was just trying to project on to me?

Except that he was right.

Even worse, I loved him. Completely. We had spent such a short time together but every moment had seemed so intense. Like we crammed all the stages of a relationship into a week.

I had to get him back.

And Marisol—I could kill her. She claimed to have been trapped by the press and that she was in fact telling them that I actually liked him despite his scars but they misquoted her. If Grady never took me back, I would never forgive her.

I plugged my phone into the car and pressed the button for my ballroom mix, long hidden from my ears. First song that came on was a foxtrot, "You're Nobody Till Somebody Loves You." Dean Martin's soothing voice penetrated deep into my soul. Memories flashed back of competing at Blackpool in England, Pasha leading me around the floor, the crowd screaming our number, my mom shouting louder than everyone.

Grady was right. I missed dancing—not the drama, not the show, but dancing. When my mom died, I'd banished that entire part of my life. It took being around a man who'd lost his own dream to realize how my own heart ached for mine.

I pulled over at the next shopping area and set my eyes on a coffee shop. But I had something important to take care of first.

One last dance, for me, for Grady. Maybe if he could see me face my fears, he could conquer his.

I dialed the numbers, my hands shaking.

"Hello?"

Benny. I hadn't heard his voice in years. My former mentor. My master coach. Benny held one link to my past. A past I refused to ignore anymore.

"Benny, it's Isa. I'm ready to dance again. Is there anyway you can find a place for me on the show?"

GRADY

I was alone in this amazing but now tainted house, the scent of Isa still lingering in the air. I was due back on base for my next round of treatments by tomorrow. Useless treatments that hadn't helped me at all.

Had Isa meant what she'd said? That she not only loved me but thought that we could have a beautiful life together? Even if she'd told me the truth about what she'd said to her friend, the damage was done.

And she baited me. "But I'm going to do something about it." I'd once been a leader; men followed my orders, lived and died by my decisions, they entrusted me with their lives.

A leader takes action, fixes what's wrong, and doesn't sit around and give up.

I'd never look the way I had before the war, but I could be that man again.

I logged into the computer and searched around, finding a list of residential treatment programs I'd been referred to. I'd always refused to even consider attending in the past. But experiencing a glimpse of happiness with Isa made me want to see if I could really heal.

After an hour of searching, one program stood out to me. Thirty days, on a working ranch, hunting, fishing, living off the land. Of course there was the usual bullshit, daily therapy, group and individual.

Once I saw the price tag, my hopes were dashed. But I knew I needed this. I'd find a way. Maybe when I finished treatment, I could start over with Isa. But I wasn't doing this for her, or even as a way to get her back, I was doing this for me.

BELLA

*B*enny had pulled some strings, and I'd been asked to come on the show as a member of the troupe. The troupe. A backup dancer to younger dancers. Dancers I'd trained. But I had no problem eating my humble pie. This gift helped me in two ways—I needed the money and it would also provide me a way to heal my soul. Reconnect with dancing. Fall back in love with the passion that had consumed my life.

I hadn't danced in years, and I was grateful for this opportunity.

Benny Brooks, my larger-than-life former coach and resident jerk judge, strolled into the studio wearing a purple suit with a black dress shirt and a bolo tie. At almost sixty, the self-proclaimed Silver

Fox still commanded a room and even had recently married a dancer forty years his junior.

"Isa, luv, I knew you'd be back. That was surer than a bum in the bucket."

I laughed as he embraced me and gave me the required cheek kiss. I'd missed his crass Australian humor. "Thank you for giving me the opportunity."

"Well, that's not all, lassie. I read that you're involved with that hero, that soldier."

Great. Grady was right, the story had gone viral. "He's a Marine, not a soldier."

"Right. We've been after him for a year to come on the show. Maybe you could sway him?"

Ha! That was almost laughable. "He's not even speaking to me now."

And that was the truth. Grady had gone radio silent. My texts went unanswered, my calls went straight to voicemail. Even his Facebook page was offline. Nothing. It was like he had vanished from the world, like he'd only been a figment of my imagination.

Benny started to say something, but I tuned him out as an idea hit me.

"Actually, Benny, maybe I can reach him. Will you let me dance a tribute to him on a show?"

Benny squinted his eyes. "Of course, luv. We can

do sometime in the next few weeks if you like. Just let me know what you need."

I squealed and hugged him. I couldn't wait to choreograph a dance for Grady. Show him with my body what I hadn't been able to say with words.

But how could I make sure he'd be watching? I quickly hatched a plan.

I picked up my phone and called a reporter—the same reporter who had written that horrible article about him.

After leaving a quick voicemail, my phone rang.

"Miss Applebaum, thank you for reaching out to me. Did you want to go on record regarding Grady Williams?"

"Yes. I did. Yes, we had a deal, but along the way, I fell in love with him. Grady's the most heroic, romantic, and sexy man I've ever met. I love him. I'm dancing a tribute for him in a future show. Please make sure to include that."

I answered some more questions and agreed to send him pictures of Grady and me.

This plan had to work. He would see the article, and hopefully, see me dance.

GRADY

*T*he blue sky had threads of purple and amber running through it. Sunset approached, but for the first time in years, I wasn't scared.

I'd been in Montana for the past four weeks, riding horses, taking care of the farm animals, and inhaling the fresh air.

I missed Isa. Her smile, her warmth, her love. We'd had no contact at all, and I wondered if she had tried to get in touch with me. But I wasn't allowed a cell phone, internet access, or even the daily newspaper here, and I loved being disconnected from the world.

But not from her.

The more time I had away from her, the more I realized how much I loved her, no matter how ridiculous that sounded. We'd spent a week together, an amazing week. But we'd been together twenty-four hours a day, and I'd opened up to her more than I'd ever opened up to anyone. In addition to her physical beauty, she was compassionate and was able to see me for me. And I loved her feisty personality, the way she called me on my bullshit, trying to make me a better man. She made me want to be a better man.

I'd do whatever I could to get her back. Glimpses of myself pre-accident started reappearing in my personality. Could she love the badass Marine instead of the fucked up vet? Time would tell.

"Hey, Grady. Pull up a seat." Ben, a fellow Marine with PTSD, hovered around the television. We were allowed to watch one hour a week of TV, and since we didn't get any access to porn, Ben had decided *Dancing under the Stars* was the closest alternative.

"Nope, not interested. My girl used to be on that show." My girl, was she still my girl? Was she ever?

"Yeah? Which one?"

And then, as if my eyes were deceiving me, Isa's incredible body appeared on the screen. Not a clip from an old show, but live. Her hair was now jet-black, her skin was tanner, but luckily she hadn't lost any of her luscious curves.

"That one."

The announcer spoke: "And join us next week for

a special treat when two-time *Dancing under the Stars* winner, Bella Applebaum, will be dancing a special tribute to an American Hero, Sergeant Grady Williams."

What the fuck?!

The show showed an old clip of her dancing with Pasha, that jackass leading her around the floor. I wanted to kill the motherfucker for ever touching her.

"Damn, dawg. She's fucking hot. Look at those fucking legs. Did you hit that?"

"I'm about to hit you if you don't shut the fuck up."

But I couldn't blame the boy; Isa was hot. Gorgeous. She teased me with glimpses of her thighs, her gown seemed to be painted on her incredible ass, and her chest glistened in the glow of the spotlight.

"Dude, I'm out."

I went back to my room to pack, my treatment was up this week anyway.

I had to go get my girl.

GRADY

J arrived in Los Angeles feeling strong and confident. Turns out, Isa had given an interview to a reporter talking about her relationship with me and clarifying that she was in no way repulsed by me.

I'd secured VIP tickets to the show and an all-access pass to the back lot. My truck pulled into the back gate at the television studios, and I shook my head as I took it all in. I'd been on a few news shows after receiving my medals, but those shows were nothing like this Hollywood mind fuck. *Dancing under the Stars* had a huge lot, trailers for makeup, hair, and the "celebrity guests." The trailers reminded me of war bunkers, and my anxiety was on high alert.

Taking a deep steadying breath, I parked and walked toward the dressing trailers.

Before I'd even walked ten feet, I instantly recognized Pasha. He stopped mid-stride when he saw me. This time his hair was wavy and scrunched together in a man bun. He sported a face full of stubble and was dressed in gray sweat pants and a too-tight white T-shirt. He looked like a member of a 90s boy-band.

I held my cool, imagining Isa being fondled by this guy. How he'd touched her thighs when they'd danced. How he'd called me a freak.

"Allo, Grady. Welcome. I want to apologize to you. I was out of line. No hard feelings."

He stuck his hand out, but I refused his handshake.

"I am sorry about what I said to you in Tahoe. You're the man! I can't believe it that you jumped on the bomb. That's crazy, bro. Bella won't shut up about you."

"It wasn't a bomb, it was a grenade."

"That's cool." He lit a cigarette and it caught me off guard. Didn't dancers take care of their bodies? I expected that shit out of my Marines, but not this guy.

"Let me get Bella for you."

"No. She doesn't know I'm here. I want it to be a surprise."

"Okay, man. She will be around here. I can take you somewhere to hide until show time."

Why was he being so cool to me? This guy was a snake—I'd already seen his true colors and I didn't trust him at all. But I didn't want Isa to see me before the show. "Sure, that would be great. I really appreciate it."

"You're welcome. And tonight you will see Isa dance together with me. But I assure to you, it is just dance."

The rage built in my chest. She was dancing with this motherfucker? After what he had said to me? Some loyalty.

Pasha stared at me, as if he was trying to read my face. "No, no, man. It is not like that. We were partners, for years. The fans, they want to see us one more time. She's crazy about you. There is nothing going on together with us. And I'm really sorry about that day I came at you. I was wrong. Bella, she is like my kid sister, and she grew up. I was jealous."

"It's fine, man." It still pissed me off, but I realized she probably hadn't had a choice. Either way, I had to go with my gut—this guy was full of shit. When I'd met him, he'd been a dick to Isa and me. Now it seemed he was going out of his way to convince me that he didn't like Isa and that he thought I was a good guy? Sorry. I wasn't buying what he was selling.

He led me to a room on the floor above the stage. "Stay in here. The dancers will be walking down the hallway. Before we go on, I'll bring you down to VIP sitting area. She won't see you until she dances. It will be in a few hours. Can I get you something? Water? Something to eat?"

"Sure."

He put his hand on my shoulder. "Don't even mention it, seriously. I know I'm just dancer, but I love America. Back in Russia, I used to dream of coming to here. I am refugee; I was beaten in the streets. My parents risk our lives to come to here. Men like you are why we are free. I thank you for your service."

Whoa. Over the years, so many people had thanked me for being a Marine, for risking my life. But most of them had been American born. Hearing Pasha's appreciation for the military choked me up. But I couldn't shake the feeling that he was plotting something, though I was sure that my therapist and Isa would say that I was paranoid. "Thanks, man."

"I wish I had your courage. When Bella was teen, her mom died. I didn't help her. I was too scared of ruining my own career and pissed off at her for leaving me. I'm glad she has a man like you. I'll be back in a few minutes with your food and drink." He walked out the door leaving me to deal with the whiplash he'd just given me.

I sat in the empty room with its dirty carpet and tiny windows. Even just a few months ago, this isolation could've sent me into a complete panic attack. But I felt better, definitely not healed, but calm.

For the last month in rehab, I'd pondered living with a new reality. Looking toward the future instead dwelling on the past. Maybe I would enjoy sharing my story with people, inspiring them. Maybe it wasn't so bad to be deemed a hero.

BELLA

*T*he tribute to Grady was tonight and my legs were restless. What had I been thinking? Of course he wouldn't see it. The guy clearly hated my guts. I still hadn't heard a word from him since I'd left him standing in the driveway of the cabin. I couldn't believe how much of a fool I'd been.

But at least my luck was changing. With the money from this season, I'd actually be able to afford to finish college next semester.

Dancing under the Stars had changed so much from when I'd been on it. Now it was all about the drama— fake fights between the judges and dancers, showmances, and scandals. And the dancers were now treated as celebrities.

I emerged from the production trailer, shaking at the

thought of reentering my own world. My skin sparkly, my dress sequined, my nerves shot. The sun blinded me, illuminating me in a beam, like maybe an alien would abduct me from this place. Maybe I hoped it would.

I walked toward the sound stage.

I was sure the public thought that this show was filmed on some glamorous set, but that couldn't be further from the truth. We were housed in a studio in the back of the lot that resembled a high school auditorium. The audience members were sandwiched into chairs around the stage, and the "ballroom" wasn't even regulation size, which made it impossible to dance a decent waltz. Last time I'd danced here, the show had this amazing live band, true musicians to play our songs. Always warmed my heart and reminded me of my favorite competition, Blackpool in England—the only competition where we danced to live music. But the TV band had been fired, and we would now be forced to dance to crappy prerecorded songs. This decision was the result of the producers' cheap iron fist and the sinking ratings of this show that had overextended its shelf life by five years.

Would Grady be watching me tonight? Somewhere silently connecting with me? My heart hurt. I was convinced he was avoiding me, but I held out hope he was somewhere getting the treatment he needed. I refused to give up hope on us until I could speak with him.

The haunting sounds of the show's opening number played over the speakers. My time was here. One featured dance, one rumba, for Grady, for my fans, for me. My official goodbye to the ballroom. Last time, I'd just quit mid-season. This time, I'd do it right. Even if Grady wasn't watching me live, he would be with me when I stepped onto the floor.

Pasha came behind me and squeezed my hand. "You look beautiful, Bella. You're going to do great tonight."

I gritted my teeth. Since we'd been back on set, he'd been overly nice to me, apologizing for how he'd behaved in Tahoe. And though he'd repeatedly asked me out, I'd told him that I was only interested in Grady. I had begged Benny to let me dance with another partner, but this was the only way he would allow me to do the spotlight. And I understood—to so many people in the ballroom world we were Pashabella. A championship couple. United through dance. They wanted to see us dance together, and this would be the last chance they had.

"And now, for the first time in four years, two-time *Dancing under the Stars* champion, Bella Applebaum, and her former partner, Pasha Gravilov."

Pasha led me onto the floor, and the lights dimmed.

Last time, I'd danced had been for my mother. She'd sat in the front row of the show, her cheeks glowing from the incandescent lights. When I'd received a perfect ten, she'd beamed at me, so proud. I remember thinking she was so beautiful, her red dress clung to her curves, her long, black hair curled at the end.

I almost wished that had been my last memory of her.

The music began, "Grenade" by Bruno Mars. It was an acoustic version that had been reworked into a classic slow rumba, soothing, melodic. The perfect song for Grady.

Pasha pushed me into a back break and pulled me back into him. My head rested on his chest as my feet did swivels on the floor. My soul soared as he spun me out to fan. As my eyes grazed the audience, there in the limelight I saw Grady.

I almost stopped dancing. He looked so handsome, and completely out of his element. He was dressed in a fitted suit, his eye gleaming, and a rare smile on his face. I struggled to continue, but Pasha saved me, pulling me back into him, guiding my body into the movements, presenting me to the audience, showing me off to the only man who mattered.

This song, this dance evoked exactly how I felt about Grady. I loved him, I'd do anything for him. He was the most selfless, kind man I'd ever met. All I wanted was to be his.

Pasha gripped my thighs, throwing me into a split, acting as the perfect frame for my picture. When the music died down, the roar of the applause drowned me.

I looked back up to meet Grady's stare. He was standing, clapping harder than anyone, his scars accented by the bright camera in his face. *Ay dios mío! No!* The camera director was focused on him. They probably intended to make it a clip for the show. How horrifying! I had no idea he'd be here.

Pasha quickly led me off the floor, away from Grady, and gave me a kiss on the top of my hair.

"You were amazing, Bellichka. Are you sure you don't want to compete together with me one more time?"

"Positive. But thank you, I couldn't have done it without you."

"You need to go back to your dressing room. I think you have a surprise waiting."

He knew? Had Grady contacted him to get on set? Maybe Pasha had set this up as a way to apologize to me?

After making my way through the maze backstage,

ALANA ALBERTSON

I ran to my trailer, anxious to jump into Grady's arms. I pushed past security and saw the door to my trailer ajar. He must've run in first.

"Grady?"

My trailer seemed empty. I heard running water in the shower. Maybe Grady was waiting for me to join him? I couldn't wait to rub my hands all over his rock solid body, kiss his face, tell him how much I'd missed him.

But when I opened the bathroom door, no one was there.

And the shower was on.

What in the world?

The loud slam of my trailer door chilled me.

I stepped out of the bathroom, praying to be reunited with Grady, but instead Pasha was standing in front of the door, holding a gun.

I screamed, but he pointed the gun at my head.

"You're mine, Bellichka. All mine. You ruined our partnership, you ruined my life. We spent years training and you tossed me aside. All I ever wanted was you. Now you're going to pay. No way are you going to choose a monster over me."

GRADY

The crowd was heavy and the room was stuffed with equipment. A few reporters came at me, but I blew them off. The only person I wanted to see was Isa.

Watching her dance, in her element, made me truly appreciate her beauty. But more than that, I was overwhelmed that she had dedicated a dance to me. I now believed what she'd told me all along—she wasn't repulsed by me; she was in awe of me. Though Pasha's slimy hands on my woman repulsed me, I knew in my heart that I was the only man on her mind.

I'd be reunited with my woman in minutes. The anticipation of wrapping my arms around her, this time vowing to never let her go, invigorated me. I walked out of the set toward the dressing trailers, when I heard a scream.

It was Isa.

Fuck.

I bolted toward the dressing trailers. Which one was hers? The others were labeled but there were some that were unmarked. I didn't have time to waste. I kicked down the door of the first one—no sign of Isa. I sprinted to the next one, busting in, but again, my girl wasn't there.

"Isa!" I called out, hoping she would respond.

But I heard nothing but the silence of the night. Which meant only one thing.

She couldn't speak.

Three more trailers broken into and I still hadn't found her. I finally came to one at the corner of the lot. One swift kick and I'd hit the jackpot.

I'd found my girl.

Pasha was on top of Isa, his dick pressed against her thigh, one hand rubbing her breast, one hand holding a gun. Her body was stark naked, stripped for this pervert.

Hell no!

Bile rose in my throat. I was going to kill this guy.

"Grady, be careful! He has a gun!"

My own gun was in the glove compartment of my truck. But I didn't need a gun. I wasn't afraid of this motherfucker. I'd seen combat. I'd fought with the real enemies. And I'd won.

"Get the fuck off her; this is your only warning."

The asshole laughed, fucking laughed, at me. He stood up—his pencil thin dick waving at me.

"What are you going to do, freak? Fight me?" His eyes seemed to be a darker shade of blue and his pupils were dilated.

"Yup. What does shooting me accomplish? You go to jail and never see Isa again. Put down the gun and let's have a fair fight. The better man wins."

I glared at Isa, praying she could read my mind. I needed her to remain calm until I could unarm this psycho.

His gun was now pointed toward my chest.

"I am not going to fight together with you, you monster. Turn around and walk out of here so I can have my way with my girl. Or you can stay and watch, if that is your thing." He turned to Isa. "It didn't have to be like this. All I ever want is to be pleasing to you."

I mouthed, "Go with it," to Isa.

She touched his waist. "You are. Let me show you how much I want you, how much I always wanted you."

"You mean it?"

"Yes, Pashka. It's always been you. Since we were kids, I dreamed of this day. You know how much I wanted you." She caressed his hand and kissed him on the lips, and his grip on the gun looked shaky.

This had gone on long enough. I ran toward him and lunged at his neck, pulling him off of Isa.

Isa grabbed the gun and pointed it at Pasha.

Cocking my arm back, I punched him square in the face, knocking him out cold.

As Pasha slumped to the floor, I secured the weapon from Isa.

"Did he hurt you?" I wrapped my arms around her, her body shivering.

"No, he just touched me. Scared me. You got here in time." Her voice cracked. "This is all my fault. Pasha, going on the show. How did I not see this coming? I just want to go away with you. You're all I have."

In this fucked-up moment, her words provided me comfort. She was still my girl. "Hey, listen to me. This is not your fault. That guy was clearly a psycho. I'm never going to leave you again, baby. I've got you. I love you."

Isa was shaking, her body cold to my touch. I helped Isa dress, called 911, and within minutes, police cars had surrounded the trailer, with studio security finally deciding to show up. Useless fuckers.

We were hauled down to the station to give our

statements, and after what seemed like hours of questioning, Isa and I were finally free to go. Together.

"I don't want to be alone tonight. Or ever. Can I stay with you?"

I kissed her on the forehead, and gently stroked her hair. "Of course, baby. I'm never letting you out of my sight."

GRADY

My first goal was to get somewhere we could be alone. Safe. Together. We checked into a nearby hotel and I hoped we could start putting this nightmare behind us...

Once in the room, she kept her distance from me and shifted on her feet. "I can't believe you showed up. Where were you all this time? I called you, texted you, messaged you. Nothing."

I was pleasantly surprised she'd been so persistent trying to get a hold of me, especially since I'd told her that I never wanted to see her again. "I'm sorry. I couldn't contact you. I was in rehab. No phones, no internet."

Her mouth gaped and her shoulders relaxed. "Really? Oh my God, Grady, I was hoping that's where you were, but I didn't believe you'd actually go. Do you feel any better?"

I walked over to her and held her waist, staring into her eyes. "Yeah, actually I do. It was rough, but some of the therapies made me feel better. Made me realize that I needed to go after what I wanted and not be stuck in the past. It helped to meet guys I could relate to on a deeper level, who understood what I was going through. Then I saw that you were going to dance for me on TV. So I left to come find you."

Her hand reached up and caressed my skin. "Now I feel bad. Were you ready to leave? I can take you back there and wait for you until you're done."

"No. I'm good." I cupped her cheeks in my hands and kissed her face. Just a loving kiss. Nothing more. She had been through enough today. "I don't want to be away from you again." For the first time, I saw her completely differently. She wasn't a sex object to me anymore, she was a beautiful woman who I wanted to make happy.

I wrapped her in my arms and clutched her to my chest. "Let's get some rest. I'm taking you somewhere special tomorrow."

"Where?"

Had she already forgotten about the ball? "It's a surprise."

ISA

*T*he next morning, he woke me before sunrise. "Let's go."

I glanced at my phone to check the time. "Now? It's four in the morning. We've only slept a few hours."

"Now, sleeping beauty."

I yawned and sat up in bed, trying to focus. "I was hoping to spend all day in bed." I'd missed him so much. I just wanted to make love to him all day, order room service, and watch some movies.

"Ha. Don't tempt me. Get up, we're going to be late."

I hated surprises. "Late? For what?"

He had a devilish smirk on his face. "I told you, it's a surprise."

"Fine." I didn't know what he was up to but I reluctantly packed our bags, and we headed back to the truck. He drove on the freeway, and he pulled into LAX. Long-term parking.

"Grady, what's going on?" My nerves were jittery.

"The ball? Remember? You promised."

"You're taking me to Hawaii?" I couldn't believe I'd forgotten that the ball was today. I'd put it out of my mind after Tahoe. I was thrilled that we hadn't missed it.

"Yup. Let's go."

Ay dios mío! I squealed and jumped into his arms. We kissed and his hands ran down my back, caressing my body. I wanted more but he placed me down, and we headed into the airport. My heart sang, and I couldn't resist humming. Yesterday had been one of the scariest days of my life, the other being when my mom died, but twenty-four hours later I was happier than I'd ever been. My beast had returned to me.

Five hours later, and one too many mai tais, our plane touched down. My mouth was watering in anticipation of eating my weight in chocolate-covered macadamia nuts. But more than anything, I was eager to get Grady alone in the hotel.

We climbed into a taxi, but when we arrived at the hotel, Grady just took our bags and instructed me to wait.

A few minutes later, he returned. "Ala Moana, please."

"The mall? We just got here. Can't we relax?"

"No. The ball's tonight and you need a dress and heels. I didn't think we'd make it, but I already have my blues ready—they were sent to the room."

"Tonight? It's two o'clock? I need to get my hair and makeup done."

"I know this. Don't worry, baby. I've got it taken care of. Let me spoil you."

As we drove down to the mall, my head spun. Within twenty-four hours, I'd gone from wondering if I would ever see Grady again, to spotting him in the audience, to almost being raped by Pasha, to end up in Hawaii, about to attend a ball, and meet the President. And I couldn't believe Grady had offered to take me on a shopping spree. No man had ever done anything this nice for me.

"Where to?" he asked.

I never spent money on clothes. I didn't go anywhere, really, besides school. "You really don't have to do this, Grady."

He put his hand on my back. "Let's go here." He pointed at Bloomingdale's.

We walked into the store and took the escalator to the second floor. An older sales clerk approached us, her eyes immediately focusing on Grady.

"Sergeant Grady Williams? It's an honor. My son is a Marine. Thank you for your service, son."

Whoa. We hadn't been in public for more than a few minutes. Did this always happen to Grady? It was really starting to seem like it.

"Thank you, ma'am. My girlfriend is trying to find a dress for the Marine Corps Ball. Very formal. Could you help her?"

Girlfriend. First time he'd said it to anyone in public. I loved the way it sounded.

"Of course, I'd be honored." She turned her attention to me. "Do you have any particular style or color in mind?"

I shrugged. "No, I'm not sure what's in style."

"That's fine, dear." She surveyed my body, guessing correctly my size, and brought out a selection of dresses.

The weight of last night's attack still heavy on my mind, I wanted something simple and classy. My eyes immediately went toward a navy blue A-line dress with a lace bodice, sweetheart neckline, empire waist, and a layered chiffon skirt. I pulled the dress over my head, the soft fabric draping across my curves. I gasped when I saw myself in the mirror. The dress was stunning.

I walked out of the dressing room, and Grady did a double take when he saw me.

He walked over to me and kissed my cheek. "You look gorgeous."

That was easy. I changed out of the dress, and in the rest of our shopping whirlwind, he also bought me heels and a clutch. Before I knew it, he'd dropped me off at a spa, where they did my nails, hair, and makeup.

I felt like a princess.

Two hours later, my jaw dropped, literally dropped, when he picked me up in his full dress blues, medals gleaming, especially the Medal of Honor around his neck. The sight of his scars never made me wince anymore. As far as I could see, he was the sexiest man alive.

"Hello, handsome."

He took my arm and led me to a limo parked outside.

Once inside, Grady poured himself a glass of whisky and I had a rum and coke. It was as if we were going to prom, another experience I'd skipped because of my dancing.

The limo took us to the Hawaiian Marriott.

I stopped for a moment to take in the view of the beach and the palm trees, the scent of freesias in the air. We walked upstairs to the ballroom, all eyes staring at us. I'd had the public eye on me before, but never on the arms of someone I loved. Who I was proud of. Who I wanted to spend the rest of my life with. And as if this night couldn't get any better, I was about to meet the President.

GRADY

I straightened my medals, and put my arm around Isa's back. Six months ago, I'd doubted that I would ever even find a date to take to the ball. Now I was here attending with the most breathtaking woman, inside and out. And better yet, she loved me.

The place was swarmed with secret service men, another career I'd wanted to consider after being a sniper. But I shook it off, refusing to focus on what couldn't be.

A bunch of Devil Dogs greeted us, including my best friends, Beau, Diego, Preston, and Trace. I beamed with pride after introducing Isa, as my girl-friend, to them. After catching up my men, Isa and I posed for formal pictures.

ALANA ALBERTSON

The commandant walked over. I'd met him once when I'd been awarded my medal. "Good evening, sir. I'd like you to meet my girlfriend, Isa Cuesta."

"Good evening, Sergeant. Nice to meet you, miss. Sergeant Williams, the President has requested your presence. Please join us."

We were escorted to the back table where the President was sitting with a few other high-ranking Marines. He stood up when he saw me. "Sergeant Williams, it's lovely to see you again. And who is your beautiful date?"

I shook his hand. "This is my girlfriend, Isa Cuesta."

The President kissed Isa's hand. "It's an honor, Mr. President," she said shyly.

"The honor is mine. Sergeant Williams tells me you're a dancer. I hope to see you dance tonight."

She bit her lip adorably. "Oh, I'd love to. I'm so happy to be here."

The ball was about to start so we were seated for the Commandant's Birthday Message. A video played, showing the history of the Marine Corps. I was interviewed in the reel, cringing when I saw myself on the high definition screen.

"I'm Sergeant Grady Williams. I'm a Marine. And Marines will do anything for each other. Semper Fidelis. Always Faithful. I didn't think I was going to die that day, I knew I was going to. But if I could've saved one life, I knew my sacrifice was worth it."

Isa's eyes welled with tears, and she clutched my hand. Her fingers looked so delicate placed in my white gloves.

The video ended, and there was the cutting of the Marine Corps cake, as well as a presentation recognizing the oldest Marine, a Korean War vet who was eighty-five, and the youngest Marine, a seventeen-year-old private.

I was having a blast, drinking, eating our catered dinner, seeing all my friends again.

Once dinner was over, an announcer took the stage.

Nerves overtook me. I had another surprise for Isa.

"And now we have a special treat. Sergeant Williams, please take the floor."

"What?" she turned to me and I stood up and led Isa out to face the audience.

The sweat dripped down my face as I clung to Isa. Strobe lights, people packed into the audience like sardines. I spied my friends at their tables, dressed in their dress blues, clapping their hands manically. Man, what had I done?

"And now, dancing a slow foxtrot to 'Tale as Old as

Time,' our guest of honor, Sergeant Grady Williams and Isa Cuesta."

The audience roared. The blue dress hugged her incredible curves. And I didn't need a mask or a costume. I was a beast. Her beast.

She back led me through the song as I tried to focus on doing heel leads and keeping the rhythm slow, quick, quick, slow. I hated to admit it, but I actually enjoyed dancing—the pressure of Isa's tight body on mine, the softness of her skin in my scarred hands as we moved as one to the music. I was in complete control. Of the dance, of her, and of my life.

After a few more steps, she twirled off me in a flourish of a finish. My Marines stood up, their claps and catcalls deafening.

She kissed my lips. "I can't believe you danced with me."

I lowered my hands to her waist and kissed her back. As the applause continued around us, I reached into my breast pocket, and pulled out a ring. I had a question to ask her.

ISA

*B*efore I could even realize what Grady was doing, he'd dropped to one knee in front of me, holding a ring. I thought I was going to faint.

"I love you, Isa. I want you to be my wife. Will you marry me?"

What? A day ago I thought I'd never seen him again. He looked up at me, his face so hopeful, yet strong and confident. We had so much to talk about, so much to work out. Were we ready for this?

I took a deep breath. We would figure out all the details later. All I knew was that I wanted to be with his man forever.

"*Ay dios mío,* Grady. Yes!"

He picked me up and kissed me. Applause rang out through the banquet room.

I stared at my ring, a beautiful oval-cut diamond set in rose gold.

Rose.

From my beast.

My beast. My prince. My hero.

My fiancé.

EPILOGUE

For my final act in the Marine Corps, I married my lovely bride in a traditional Marine Corps wedding, my buddies creating the arch with their swords.

After Isa and I were married, our lives had blended together seamlessly. She'd re-enrolled in her senior year at UCSD, and I found a job working with wounded warriors, men and women just like myself. It was great to know that I could inspire those who felt as desperate and despondent as I once had.

I'd decided not to write the war memoir with her father because I wanted to avoid the media spotlight, especially since we were starting our lives together. Isa understood, especially after I confessed to her that the only reason I had agreed to the book in the first place was to get close to her. But I did introduce my father-in-law to a fellow wounded warrior and they had agreed to collaborate on a book together. With his new book deal, he was able to save the house. Isa's relationship with her old man was strained, but he was making an effort to repair the damage he caused by stealing her trust fund.

Money was tight, but we were both fine living on a budget. Between Isa's job teaching dancing, and my income from my job and the VA, we would make ends meet.

Pasha had been arrested and charged with kidnapping and attempted rape. Because he had no priors he pled it down to probation. I'd always known there was something seriously off about that guy. Turns out, he had pending allegations of sexual assault with other dance students. They had been afraid to file a report against a TV star. He must've counted on Isa being an easy target. But instead she pointed the gun at his head. Isa was strong and beautiful.

I would never stop missing Rafael, but I finally found some comfort, knowing he would want me to be happy, and that he was guarding the gates of heaven.

Almost a year after we met, I looked out the window of our apartment and heard the sounds of a party from the local frat house where Isa and I had met.

"Hey, there's a party down there. Looks like some superhero theme. Would you like to go?"

Isa came over to me and wrapped her arms around my neck as I squeezed her ass.

"I'd love to. But this time, let's go as the Joker and Harley Quinn. You don't need a mask."

Thank you for reading The Beauty and The Beast!

I hope you loved Grady and Isa. Catch up with them and meet their friends, Erik and Aria in The Mermaid and The Triton—A Navy SEAL Little Mermaid Retelling!

I'm a Navy SEAL, a Triton, a god of the sea.
And she will never be part of my world.

Available now: Book 2 in the Heroes Ever After Series
The Mermaid and The Triton

ONE CLICK The Mermaid and The Triton now!

And sign up for my *newsletter* to find to get my book
Deadly Sins FOR FREE!

Turn the page for an excerpt from
The Mermaid and The Triton
XOXO
Alana

THE MERMAID AND THE TRITON

CHAPTER 1 ERIK

A Navy SEAL Little Mermaid Retelling

Aria—I teach mermaid fitness at a ritzy hotel next to the Naval Amphibious Base. I know better than to let one of those famous frogmen chase my tail. But in a moment of weakness, I submit to Erik, a tattooed badass Navy SEAL. After one night of incredible passion, I can't stop thinking about his cocky ways and his dirty mouth.

Then I get the opportunity to train to be the first female Navy SEAL.

When I show up on the first day of training, I'm horrified to realize that Erik is my BUD/S instructor. He's the only person who stands in the way of me achieving my dream.

I'm no quitter. He can taunt me, tease me, and run me ragged, but I'll never ring that bell.

Erik—Aria is the most incredible woman I've ever met. She won the gold medal for synchronized swimming and she looks like a little mermaid the way she moves underwater. Once I find out that the sexy redhead is teaching aquatic classes next to my base, I vow to do anything to make her mine.
After our mind-blowing night together, she vanishes. I ask around and learn she went away to train. I assume it's for another synchro competition.
I'm dead wrong.
She shows up in BUD/S as part of the first class to let in women. I'm head instructor of Phase One, and there's no way in hell I will lower the standards of my Team to please the brass and make a political statement.
It doesn't matter how much I want her because she's forbidden to me now. I'm the teacher and she's my student. She will obey my every command.
She can try to pass hell week but she will fail.
I'm a Navy SEAL, a Triton, a god of the sea.
And she will never be part of my world.

Chapter One—Erik

In the water, out of the water. Pain for you, fun for me.

I placed my hand over the raised motto printed on the back of my long-sleeved, dark blue instructor shirt from my locker in the BUD/S compound. Warmth filled my chest as I pulled the shirt over it.

Today was going to be epic.

It was my first day as a BUD/S instructor—responsible for training the next generation of Frogmen. Only eight years ago, I'd been a mere tadpole myself. My instructors were such badasses, and now it was my turn to inflict the hurt. After surviving many deployments with SEAL Team Seven, I had been graced with this coveted non-deployable three-year land duty. Three years stateside in beautiful Coronado, California—home to the sexiest women in the world. Yup, there were plenty of fish in the sea.

Maybe I would finally get over Aria.

My buddy Devin walked into the room. With his pretty boy swagger, long blonde hair, steel-grey eyes, and movie star smile, there was no doubt that he used to be a world-famous rock star, even though he kept his true identity a fiercely guarded secret. The guys had nicknamed him, "Skin," because, like Rumplestiltskin, he never would admit to anyone outside of the

Teams that he had once graced the cover of Rolling Stone shirtless and clad in skin tight leather pants. He had abandoned his former life as Dax, lead guitarist of Gold Whiskey, the millennium's hottest heavy metal band, to become an operator.

I couldn't fathom ever earning that much money and then giving it up. And as much as I loved my job, I struggled to accept the fact that even though I risked my life daily to protect America, on my salary, I would never be able to save enough money to buy a home where I was stationed. Any extra income I made, I sent to my mom. She was proud and humble and would always refuse to accept it, only to eventually give in reluctantly. Ever since my dad had died, she had done her best to provide for my sister but struggled to make ends meet. I was determined to help them any way I could.

Devin's hand brushed his long blonde bangs off his face. "Hey, dude. Have you seen the Frog Princess?"

Fuck. Just my fucking luck. My first time as an instructor and I had to be responsible for the downfall of the Teams. Today was the day that Naval Special Warfare would lose all its standards. Despite the Team guys' collective protests and pleas, our arguments had failed to convince the high brass of the Navy, who quite frankly didn't know shit, that having a female on the Teams was the worst idea imaginable. Fuck political correctness—I was training warriors.

I exhaled. "Nah, man. I just hope she looks like Demi Moore. Maybe we should assemble a special Team, just of women. Wait until their times of the month sync up, then deploy them. They will lay waste to the enemy."

Devin burst into laughter. "Damn straight. They could take out ISIS."

Ha! "Fuck yeah." I fastened my boots, pushed back my sunglasses, and walked around the corner, preparing to meet my class. I gazed out at the midnight blue ocean, barely visible at zero dark thirty. The waves rippled in the distance, and the scent of salt water and sweat lingered in the air. These recruits didn't have a clue what they were about to endure.

Let the games begin.

As I approached the class, my eyes were immediately drawn to the lone female in the group, as if her presence was a magnet to my cock. The tight, brown shirt clung to her breasts, and the green cammies hung low on her slender hips. Like a flame, one wisp of her red hair peeked out of her cap. She must've felt my gaze because she raised her eyes to meet mine.

Holy fuck!

My heart pounded in my chest, and my body

shook with fury.

No, she didn't look like Demi Moore. She was hotter, way fucking hotter. She wasn't anything like the type of woman I had thought would've signed up for this torture. She wasn't hardened, mean, nor did she have a chip on her shoulder.

I knew this because I knew her.

I'd loved her.

And she'd left me.

Aria stood in front of me—my little mermaid who had swum off in the middle of the night, leaving me heartbroken. She'd told me she had gone to "train." My dumb ass thought she'd meant for another shot at the Olympics. But she'd taken on the ultimate challenge.

She was here to be the first female Navy SEAL.

And I was her instructor.

I narrowed my gaze on her, purposefully intimidating her. Her chin dropped, and her eyes blinked rapidly.

My annoyance flared. What the fuck was she doing here? When had she been commissioned by the Navy? Was this why she had left me?

A tremble took over her body.

It could've been from the chill of the early morning.

Or it could've been from the horror of realizing

she had come face to face with the man she had betrayed.

A man who was now in control of every second of her life. A man who now would stand in the way of her achieving her dreams.

She had lied to me about her future plans. Used me to gain access to the SEAL "O" course. Pumped me for information about BUD/S training. But even worse, she had grown close to my family. All the while knowing that she had planned to betray me.

Now I would make her pay.

I grabbed the microphone, forcing myself to calm my voice, and looked directly at her. "Welcome to BUD/S Class 334. I'm Instructor Anderson. Many have tried, few have succeeded. Drop to the ground and give me a hundred pushups."

Before I could blink her firm, tight body was parallel to the floor as she knocked out her exercise with perfect form.

I yelled into the microphone, screaming at all of my candidates. But my mind was on only one of them.

Aria.

Her sweet loving boyfriend no longer existed. It was time to introduce her to the badass Navy SEAL she had pissed off.

The warrior. The savage. The killer.

I stood behind her, my eyes focused on her firm ass.

"Eight. Nine. Ten. You think you can do this, Clements? That you are as strong as these men? You aren't. I'll tell you what you are. You're sad. You're weak. You're pathetic. This is Navy SEAL training, not water ballet. You screw up, and I'll catch you every time. I'll make you pay, princess. I'll make you pay."

"Yes, Instructor Anderson."

I got in her face. "Don't you speak. I didn't give you permission to speak. Keep that mouth of yours shut unless I tell you to open it." *To suck my cock.*

Dammit. My mind flashed to her on her knees taking me deep. Well, one of the SEAL mottos was, "Welcome the SUCK with a big hug and a smile on your face."

Fuck. I had to stop thinking about her like that.

It didn't matter how much I had once wanted her because she was forbidden to me now. I was her instructor, and she was my student.

From now on, she would obey my every command.

From now on, I was her master.

I stepped away, and she took a quick rest on her forearms. I turned right back toward her. "When I walk away, I'll still be watching you. I have eyes on the back of my head. If I tell you to do something, you do it right. If I tell you to do pushups, you do them right. Got it, cupcake?"

She grunted, and I walked away from her, trying to focus on any of the other men, any of the candidates but her.

How had I been so wrong about her? No wonder she had become so angry when I had told her I didn't think women should be SEALs. It had once even crossed my mind that there was a possibility that she wanted to be a SEAL. But I had dismissed that thought.

I'd be the laughing stock of my Team now. Devin and Kyle both knew that I had dated her. I had to steer clear of her on our off times. Any contact with her could be misconstrued as fraternization. She had wasted enough of my life—I refused to allow her to ruin my career.

Devin yelled for them to lay on their backs and start leg lovers. I grabbed my hose and blasted a stream of water into her mouth, as her legs scissored up and down. As I counted at her, I imagined that stream of water being my cum shot into her greedy little mouth.

I dropped the hose, unable to look at the wet T-shirt clinging to her chest, her nipples poking through the damp fabric.

But on a glance back, I noticed something else. Her legs were straight, and her abs were engaged. My eyes surveyed the men on the ground. Many of them were flailing around like a fish out of water, with no form at all.

Fuck my life. She was one of the best ones in the class.

But it didn't matter. I would make her ring that bell. Her betrayal of me alone should be enough to get her kicked out.

Aria and the men completed their evolution, and I yelled at them again. "This entire evolution has been pathetic. Nothing any one of you has done has been even remotely acceptable. Maybe that's because there's a woman in your class that you have all decided to lower your standards to her level."

Her eyes tore into me, and her mouth quivered. I had to look away. I couldn't deal with her emotions.

Or mine.

But I also couldn't have anyone think that I was being extra hard on her because I'd fucked her. It wasn't just her future on the line—it was mine too.

I threw her a bone.

"But, you are all wrong. We will never lower our standards. Not for the Frog Princess or for any of you fools. And I'll tell you what. The Frog Princess showed you all up tonight. If you can't do as many leg lovers as a girl, none of the rest of you have the right to be here. 'Lady' and Gentlemen, it's going to be a long, cold, wet night."

I threw down my microphone and walked away. Inwardly, I winced— she'd made a fool out of me.

But I knew how to make her crack. How to make her doubt herself.

I knew her Achilles heel.

She would never pass the "O" course because she would never master the Dirty Name obstacle.

When I heard that sweet chime of the bell that she would ring, I would breathe a sigh of relief. For that sound would mean that I'd never have to see her again.

The sooner, the better.

She could try to pass BUD/S, but she would fail.

I was a Navy SEAL, a Triton, a god of the sea.

And she would never be part of my world.

ONE CLICK TRITON now!

And sign up for my *newsletter* to find to get my book Deadly Sins FOR FREE!

ABOUT ALANA

 ALANA ALBERTSON IS the former President of RWA's Contemporary Romance, Young Adult, and Chick Lit chapters. She holds a M.Ed. from Harvard and a BA in English from Stanford. She lives in San Diego, California, with her husband, two sons, and six rescue dogs. When she's not saving dogs from high kill shelters through her rescue Pugs N Roses, she can be found watching episodes of Cobra Kai, Younger, or Dallas Cowboys Cheerleaders: Making the Team.

Please join my newsletter to receive a free books!

Newsletter

Website

Email Me

Facebook Group

ALSO BY ALANA ALBERTSON

Want more romantic reads?

Try my other books!

Heroes Ever After

Military New Adult Fairy Tale Retellings

The Beauty and The Beast

Inspired by Beauty and The Beast

Meet Grady! With tattooed arms sculpted from carrying M-16s, this bad boy has girls begging from sea to shining sea to get a piece of his action.

The Mermaid and The Triton

Inspired by The Little Mermaid

Meet Erik! I'm a Navy SEAL, a Triton, a god of the sea. And she will never be part of my world.

The Princess & The SEAL

Inspired by The Princess and The Frog

Meet Ryan! She's a Princess and I'm a Frogman. If I kiss her, I'll turn into a Prince.

The Virgin & The Rockstar

Inspired by Rumplestiltskin

Meet Dax! All she has to do to destroy my life is to say my name.

The Maid & The Marine

Inspired by Cinderella

Meet Trace! I will never be her Prince Charming.

Rescue Me

Romantic Comedy Series

Doggy Style

Meet Preston! When it comes to doggy style, he's behind you 100%.

Blue Devils

Military Pilots Contemporary Series

Blue Sky

Meet Beckett! I'll never let down my guard for this Devil in a Blue Angel's disguise.

Blue Moon

Meet Sawyer: One Night with this Blue Devil will make you a sinner.

Se7en Deadly SEALs

Navy SEAL Romantic Thriller

Season One:

Conceit, Chronic, Crazed, Carnal, Crave, Consume, Covet

Season One Box Set

Meet Grant! She wants to get wild? I will fulfill her every fantasy.

Season Two:

Smug, Slack, Storm, Seduce, Solicit, Satiate, Spite

Meet Mitch! I'll always be your bad boy.

The Trident Code

Navy SEAL Romantic Suspense Series

Invincible

Meet Pat! I had one chance to put on the cape and be her hero.

Invaluable

Meet Kyle! I'll never win MVP, never get a championship ring, but some heroes don't play games.

Dance with Me

Swing

Meet Bret! He was a real man—muscles sculpted from carrying weapons, not from practicing pilates.

Military Contemporary Stand Alone

Badass

Meet Shane! I'm America's cockiest badass.

(co-written with *Linda Barlow*)

ACKNOWLEDGMENTS

I WOULD LIKE TO THANK the love of my life, my husband, Roger, a real Marine hero. Thank you for being such a wonderful husband to me and the best daddy to our sons. For watching the boys while I write. For keeping me caffeinated during late night writing sessions. I love you.

To Linda Barlow: for your keen editing insights, late night pep talks, and hilarious commentary. This book would've been a mess without you.

To Mia Searles: For your amazing work on the blog tour.

To Nicole Blanchard: For listening to my endless rants and encouraging (forcing) me to finish it.

To Wander Aguiar: for this amazing picture
To Andrey Bahia: for finding me the photo.

To Aria Tan: For creating this gorgeous cover.

I would like to thank my editors for turning this book into what it was meant to be:

Deb Nemeth—your endless patience reading the many different versions of this book.

Lisa Christman—for your insight into Grady's characterization.

To Julie Titus: For your amazing formatting and being such a sweet, talented person.

To my betas: Jenny Negron, Melissa Fisher, & Brittney Crabtree: thank you all for your honest critiques and making this the best story it could be.

To my two beautiful sons, Connor and Caleb for your smiles, your laughter, your hugs and kisses.

To Indie Sage Promotions for handling all the promotion for the book.

To all the fans who have written me wonderful emails. I write for you.

Made in the USA
Columbia, SC
19 August 2022

65683021R00193